NOW OR NEVER

I0682471

BRENDA BARRETT

Now or Never
A Jamaica Treasures Book/May 2017

Published by Jamaica Treasures
Kingston, Jamaica

This is a work of fiction. Names, characters, places, and incidents are either the product of the author's imagination or are used fictitiously. Any resemblance to an actual person or persons, living or dead, events, or locales is entirely coincidental.

978-976-8247-62-9
Jamaica Treasures
P.O. Box 482
Kingston 19
Jamaica W.I.
www.fiwibooks.com

"You have a boyfriend?" Randy asked belatedly.

"Yes." Addison nodded. "The timing for us is just off."

"I'd say." Randy huffed. "I don't know why I assumed you were single. Josh never mentioned to me that you were dating."

He got up and stood beside her, looking down in the fishpond. "I guess we aren't meant to be after all."

"I guess so." Addi looked at him, and her lips had a slight tremor. "I am going back to the party."

"You can break it off with him," Randy said holding her hand. "I'll wait."

Addi looked down at their joined hands and then up at Randy. The pulse in her palm was racing, and she knew her voice would be breathless. "I don't think I should."

"You should." Randy leaned toward her so close she could feel the heat from his face. She could feel his breath on her skin. "When you do, call me."

Addi inhaled tremulously and then stepped away from him. "I don't think so. Goodbye Randy."

"Never goodbye," Randy gave her a bitter half-smile, "not between you and me. I have a feeling we were meant to be

together..."

ALSO BY BRENDA BARRETT

FULL CIRCLE
NEW BEGINNINGS
THE PREACHER AND THE PROSTITUTE
AFTER THE END
THE EMPTY HAMMOCK
THE PULL OF FREEDOM
REBOUND SERIES
THREE RIVERS SERIES
NEW SONG SERIES
BANCROFT SERIES
MAGNOLIA SISTERS SERIES
SCARLETT SERIES
WILEY BROTHERS SERIES

ABOUT THE AUTHOR

Books have always been a big part of life for Jamaican born Brenda Barrett, she reports that she gets withdrawal symptoms if she does not consume at least two books per week. That is all she can manage these days, as her days are filled with writing, a natural progression from her love of reading. Currently, Brenda has several novels on the market, she writes predominantly in the historical fiction, Christian fiction, comedy and romance genres.

Apart from writing fictional books, Brenda writes for her blogs blackhair101.com; where she gives hair care tips and fiwibooks.com, where she shares about her writing life.

You can connect with Brenda online at:
Brenda-Barrett.com
Twitter.com/AuthorWriterBB
Facebook.com/AuthorBrendaBarrett

Chapter One

"So we meet again, Addi."

Addi knew it was Randy even before she turned around. She had been aware of him through the whole service and then the reception. In a room full of good-looking men he was a standout. She was sure that she was not the only female who was ogling him.

She turned around slowly from where she was to take him in fully, and then just like that, her once steady hands started to tremble on the glass of wine.

"Randy didn't see you there." She was trying for nonchalant. She failed.

"Liar." Randy laughed. "It was a nice wedding. You made a beautiful maid of honor."

"Thanks." Addi nodded. "I almost didn't show up. Sky and Travis were crazy enough to plan a large wedding in a mere two weeks."

"But you did come. It's nice to see you again." Randy cleared his throat. "Can we go somewhere quiet and talk?" He looked around the crowded poolside of the Jefferson mansion. "Maybe to the gardens?"

Addi bit her lip and then shook her head. "I don't think so. I meant what I said, Randy. I can't have a relationship with you."

"Yes, I remember," Randy nodded, "Oh, I remember last year in New York. You said I was a past mistake and that I had no place in your life this time around."

"That's right." Addi nodded. "I am glad you got the message."

"I did." Randy shrugged. "I just don't get the reason for the message."

Addi put the drink on a table and then turned around again. "Okay, come on."

Randy raised an eyebrow but did not argue. He followed her as she headed down a cobbled stone walkway all the way to a mini bridge where there was a pond and an unoccupied gazebo.

It was quite picturesque. There were koi in the pond—little colorful bodies glinting in the six o'clock sunlight. Addi stood in the gazebo her hands braced on the railing, her long curly hair in a half up half down hairdo. Her filmy long pink dress floated around her. She looked like a princess waiting for her loyal subject.

"Can I take your picture?" He asked taking out his camera; this is too lovely a moment not to capture.

Addi seemed like she thought about it for a moment and then she nodded. "Go ahead."

He snapped several shots of her and then smiled. "I guess you are used to this and all, you being a model."

"That was last year." Addi sat in one of the chairs in the gazebo. "This year I am writing a novel."

"That's quite a departure from what you said you were doing before." Randy stepped up into the gazebo and sat before her.

He loosened his bow tie and raised an eyebrow. "In the previous time, you were a doctor in sociology. You should be pursuing a masters degree by now."

"You remembered that?" Addi asked flippantly.

"I remember everything you ever told me." Randy leaned forward and frowned. "I invested in those tech stocks you told me about."

"Good for you." Addi smiled at him, the first genuine smile he was seeing from her in a while.

"I invested some of my money in real estate. After the 96 meltdown, several places were going for cheap."

"And where are you working now, or are you just investing? Addi asked him.

Interest. Finally.

Randy relaxed somewhat. "I am working at Gordon and Fletcher, chief accounting officer for their telecommunications company. That's the reason I was at the tech summit last year in New York."

"That sounds great." Addi looked at him and then away. "Really great."

"I am still not married to any pastor's daughter or have any hopes of joining the ministry." Randy reminded her of what she had told him that he had ended up doing before she had reset things.

"I am very much interested in knowing why we can't be together. You have written me off based on previous information from a timeline that I am not privy to."

Addi sighed. "I don't remember much of what happened.

I have this book where I wrote down stuff, and I cautioned myself never to get involved with you."

Randy leaned back in the chair and rubbed the back of his neck. "This is frustrating Addison. You and I have chemistry. It is stupid for us not to explore that in the here and now. I am single. You are single. I have liked you since you were a kid. Now you are a grown, gorgeous woman. You have to give us a chance."

"No!" Addi stood up. "I have other plans."

"You have a boyfriend?" Randy asked belatedly.

"Yes." Addison nodded. "The timing for us is just off."

"I'd say." Randy huffed. "I don't know why I assumed you were single. Josh never mentioned to me that you were dating."

He got up and stood beside her, looking down in the fishpond. "I guess we aren't meant to be after all."

"I guess so." Addi looked at him, and her lips had a slight tremor. "I am going back to the party."

"You can break it off with him," Randy said holding her hand. "I'll wait."

Addi looked down at their joined hands and then up at Randy. The pulse in her palm was racing, and she knew her voice would be breathless. "I don't think I should."

"You should." Randy leaned toward her so close she could feel the heat from his face. She could feel his breath on her skin. "When you do, call me."

Addi inhaled tremulously and then stepped away from him. "I don't think so. Goodbye Randy."

"Never goodbye," Randy gave her a bitter half-smile, "not between you and me. I have a feeling we were meant to be together..."

Chapter Two

January 2002

*M*oving *was like time travel, well sort of,* Addi thought staring at the stack of boxes in front of her. She just had to look into any one of them, and she could revisit some memory from a few years ago or remind herself of her past.

She pushed away a box with a bunch of her modeling pictures and then closed her eyes. Why was she even taking them with her? She didn't want to be reminded of the past, especially the last three years. She brushed the thick rope burns around her neck and shuddered.

Her life so far had been one disappointment after another, beginning with the relationship with Devin Garcia—if it could be called a relationship. He had turned out to be her worst nightmare.

She could do with a reset right now. Too bad she had already done the whole reset thing already; this would have been a perfect time to do one, but that was next to impossible. This was her life now, and she had to deal with it as best as she could. And dealing with it involved leaving New York and starting over somewhere...anywhere but here.

Her parents had visited over the Christmas holiday and had found her in the hospital looking like something the cat dragged in. Her bruises had been a bit darker and rawer looking then.

Her dad had taken one look at her and started crying. Her mother had been a bit more stoic, but Addi could see the shock on her face as well. It was no wonder that they had urged her to come home. At least for a while.

And though it felt like a backward step, what could she do? She had nothing and no one here in New York. Josh was in San Jose, California, working as a software developer. She had lost all her friends from the modeling world when she left that profession.

Her little stint as an author for the past year hadn't won her any friends. She had isolated herself from her regular church group. They had moved on especially after the media furor of last year.

She was tainted goods.

As for her book, it looked like it would be forever destined to be a manuscript. After spending nearly nine months perfecting what was in her mind—an instant best-seller, and then getting rejection after rejection from every publisher, she could no longer consider herself an author.

She couldn't do it. It wasn't the life for her.

So what was she now?

Nothing. She had a degree she had never bothered to use, and all of her excess money was gone in her pursuit of literary greatness.

She was broke, with a whole lot of nice clothes and shoes.

Boxes and boxes of shoes. Shoes she would be donating to Goodwill.

As for her relationship status, definitely single.

Single, scared and hiding from the mafia. Even now she still feared that they would come back to finish what they had started.

Addi laughed harshly to herself.

All of this because of Devin Garcia.

Devin Garcia, charismatic preacher, head of a mega church who was now languishing in federal prison because he had used his church as a front for the mafia's money laundering operation.

Her ties to Devin had almost gotten her killed because they had mistakenly assumed that she was in on his criminal activities and knew where he hid his money.

Some idiot must have mentioned that she was the ex-fiancée because she had certainly kept a low profile during the media firestorm that had taken place last year. She had holed up in her apartment, never daring to leave. Dreading the moment when someone would mention that Devin had been engaged to be married in March.

She looked at the box where she had marked wedding across the top. That was going straight to Goodwill too, with her handmade wedding souvenirs and her place settings. She had chosen a Paris themed wedding because that was where they had met in September 1999. He was on vacation with his parents and siblings, and she had been at the Paris Fashion Week. They had met by chance in a hotel lobby and had discovered that they were both from New York with Jamaican connections and the rest was easy. Devin was an easy person to be with.

She opened the box and grimaced. She had spent hours making her little Eiffel tower keepsakes. Luckily, she hadn't bought the dress or paid for the cake. She closed her eyes and envisioned the dress; it had been a lace figure hugging wedding dress, which had not been cheap. She would have to go back to the store for her deposit.

Just one of the many things that she still had to do to close this chapter in her life and move on.

She would not waste one more thought on the fact that she was on a path to nowhere. She had the golden opportunity to live her life over again, and she was doing a pathetic job of the whole thing.

Maybe if she hadn't set out exactly what she should and shouldn't do in this new version of her life things would have gone much better. Maybe, if she had just allowed herself to live, to approach her future with spontaneity and not with the kind of rigidity that she had predetermined for herself, maybe then she would be better off.

As it was, she had written a rulebook of sorts for her second time around, and it wasn't doing her any favors. She picked up the large journal, which she had on top of one of the boxes and skipped through it. She had in the very front of the book, How Not To End Up Forty, Single and Childless.

Marry early, stop nitpicking, any suitable man but Randall Vassell will do. Randy is bad news; you had a twenty-year affair with him, he has never chosen you first. You spent most of your adulthood pining for this guy, waiting for him to love you enough to choose to be with you and only you.

FORGET RANDY VASSELL!!!

Addi winced. She had that written on every page in bold. Now look at her, she had thought that she had made a head start, but it wasn't to be.

Life had curveballs. Such a pity she had not accounted for that in her black and white version of the future.

If it weren't for Mrs. Florence and her grandson across

the landing, she would be a dead person now. She would not have seen her twenty-fifth birthday. Mafia henchmen had tied her up in the apartment and tortured her about Devin's hidden money. Talk about her plans going horribly awry. How could she have foreseen that any of that would have happened?

Addi could still feel the low throbbing pain from the two cracked ribs where she had gotten a couple of blows from one of the thugs.

They had wanted answers, and she had none.

She had no clue that Devin was not a straight shooter. She thought he was a decent guy who had been romantic and restrained and thoughtful. He reminded her of her dad.

They had done the whole courtship thing right. She was going to wear white on her wedding day legitimately and then she would live happily ever after with the man who God ordained for her. And they would have children, at least four, and all of this had to happen because she was never a wife and mother before.

How could she have foreseen that in her fairytale plans, her future husband would be an undercover criminal?

Addi kissed her teeth in frustration and got up from the floor with difficulty. Her right leg was still bruised; her left ankle was still taped. She had no business being on the floor sorting through boxes. If she had any sense at all, she would not have returned to the apartment alone.

Her parents had offered to extend their holiday and help her to move, but she had refused. She had no idea what she wanted to do yet. She was still on the fence about what to do with her life.

She heard a key in the door, and she froze. She hobbled toward her bedroom. She was not going to stand in one place and wait for the unscrupulous thugs to get her again. No, no, not this time.

Obviously, she wasn't moving fast enough, the person who was coming into the apartment was already in.

"Really Addi!" It was Sky. "If you were running from me, you would be caught. You can barely hobble on your leg!"

Addi stopped and looked around at her heavily pregnant cousin. "What are you doing here? I told Mom and Dad not to tell you..."

Sky glared at her and then came fully into the apartment; she wasn't alone, Travis was behind her.

"Hi Addi," Travis said solemnly. "You look like er..."

"Like hell." Sky completed.

"Thanks." Addi relaxed slightly and then exhaled in relief. She looked between Travis and Sky. "You both look good."

Tears welled up in her eyes. "And I am glad to see you."

"Oh for heaven's sake." Sky had tears in her eyes as well. "Don't you ever hide anything from me again. Not something like this. I don't care if I am in labor. It doesn't matter where I am or what I am doing."

Sky headed for her and then clasped her in a hug, which was pretty awkward since her belly was poking between them.

"Come on let's go sit down," Sky said looking around at the crowded apartment.

Travis cleared out a settee and Addi sank down in one of them in relief.

Sky sat across from her aided by Travis.

"I can't believe what I heard." Sky squinted at her. "Tell me it's not true."

"I don't know what you heard." Addi inhaled raggedly.

"You were beaten up by thugs." Sky rounded her eyes in consternation. "Your neighbor saw the men coming in here and called the police, and her grandson kept knocking at the door asking if you were all right. The guys left by the fire escape and they found you tied to a chair, gagged and bleeding. How am I doing?"

"You sound like the news," Addi muttered.

"How can you even still be here in this place?" Sky asked. "Why would you come back?"

"I had to sort out my things." Addi shrugged. "I wasn't staying here, Mom and Dad paid for a hotel, I just came back to get my stuff. Josh is planning to sell the place anyway. I have to clear it out."

Sky nodded. "He says he is in Hong Kong for six months?"

"Yes," Addi said tiredly. "His company is doing some technological stuff that he has to oversee."

"And you are coming back to Jamaica?" Travis asked. He was sitting at the edge of the settee, watching her keenly.

"Yes." Addi grimaced. "This is a backward move though. I mean, I'll be living with my parents again. Maybe working at the hardware store. It will be just like when I was a little girl."

Sky shook her head. "You don't have to do any such thing. You can stay with us or if you don't want to you can stay in Travis' apartment. We spend all of our time at the new house anyway."

Travis nodded. "You are quite welcome to stay there, and we can find a position at the company if you want. There must be something that you would like to do there."

"I couldn't impose." Addi looked between Travis and Sky. "I mean you guys are generous and kind, but I don't want to be a family leach. You have your new baby to think about and..."

"Stop the pity fest," Sky held up her hand, "you can impose on me at any time."

She rubbed her belly absently. "You know you don't even

have to work at Jefferson Pharmaceutical; you remember Randy?"

Addi nodded slowly. What kind of question was that? She thought about Randy every day for an unhealthy amount of time. Her life up to this point was based on not wanting to repeat her history with him.

Sky knew she remembered Randy. Addi waited patiently to hear where this was going; if the sly glint in Sky's eyes was any indication, this was going to be good.

"Randy bought an insurance company," Sky said. "The other day we went to the launch. Wasn't it good, Travis?"

"It was okay." Travis shrugged. "Randy's fiancée is a little pushy. I did not get a chance to enjoy myself."

"Oh yes, she is. She is a realtor, and she is not afraid to do the hard sell. Her name is Selena Burns." Sky grimaced. "She's something else. But anyway, Randy was mentioning that he was hunting for a personal assistant, his current assistant is on the verge of retirement. He has a couple of businesses under his belt now, and he desperately wants somebody to arrange his work life."

"I wouldn't work for Randy," Addi shook her head, "It would be too awkward."

"Why?" Sky asked innocently, "it's not as if you still like him or anything. And he definitely does not like you. You should see Selena!"

"Thanks a lot," Addi growled, feeling a shaft of jealousy prick her out of nowhere.

"Oh, did I mention that the job is in Montego Bay?" Sky wrinkled her nose, "far from us but we can always fly down a couple of weekends. Randy mentioned something about accommodation, and the compensation package sounds really good. I recommended a girlfriend of mine, Emma, from university but Randy turned her down. He is very picky."

"Or, it could be that Emma is something of a handful," Travis murmured, shaking his head at Sky. "I told you Randy and Emma would not have been a good fit. The girl is practically unemployable."

"I don't think working for Randy would be a good idea..." Addi rubbed her hands together, flexing them nervously. "And I have no administration experience…"

"I would not dismiss it so readily," Sky jumped in before Addi could continue her protest. "Think about it, you might not even get it, but if you do, you wouldn't be working for family or living with Uncle Nate and Aunt Vicky. You'd be independent and who knows you may..."

Sky stopped speaking and then glanced at Travis. "Are we going to help her to pack or what? I need to make a phone call."

"Wait a minute." Addi frowned. "I don't think working for Randy would be appropriate, I mean, I..." She bit her lip.

Sky looked at her with a smug expression on her face. Waiting for her to confess that she had made a horrible decision in pushing Randy away and choosing Devin instead.

Sky's opinion was well known; she had spent half of her honeymoon two years ago, cussing out Addi about turning down Randy. So this seemingly innocent suggestion was not what it seemed on the surface.

Sky was up to something.

Addi was too banged up and feeling out of sorts to care. She would welcome a new opportunity to leave New York, like this one, even if it meant working for Randy.

"Go ahead," she sighed and pushed herself out of the sofa painfully. "It's not a bad idea. Maybe he will turn me down like he did your friend Emma."

"I doubt that." Sky fished her cell phone from her bag and

waddled to the patio.

Travis looked at Addi and then around at the room. "I know somebody who can clean up this apartment in no time."

He took out his phone and Addi was left staring into space while her life was arranged for her.

Chapter Three

"**W**hat's wrong, Randy?" Selena waved her hand in front of him and then pouted. "I feel as if I am the invisible woman."

"Sorry." Randy focused on her and then dredged up a smile. "I have a lot on my mind."

"I can see that." Selena frowned at him. "Are you going to talk to me about it, or are you going to sit there and stare into space?"

Randy dragged his mind from his latest contemplation and looked at Selena. She was still in her work clothes, a tailored pinstripe pantsuit. She had removed her jacket to reveal a peach-colored blouse that had silver rhinestones at the neck.

As usual, she was impeccably made up, her long relaxed hair was arranged in an intricate bun.

She had a no-nonsense look on her pretty face that indicated that she was more than annoyed by his absentmindedness.

"Why do I have to participate in this?" he asked, indicating to the large appointment book that Selena had spread out on her kitchen table.

"Because it is our wedding," Selena growled, "and I am not going to be the only one planning this. You need to give me some input. I need to know who we are inviting to the engagement party. It's in three weeks, Randy. The wedding planners are in my skin about the list."

"Right," Randy sighed. "But I am tired, it was a long day, and I have a ton of stuff to get done."

Selena raised an eyebrow. "I work too, you know, and the stuff I need to get done is crushingly oppressive, but that is why I have a personal assistant who is quite efficient at lessening my burdens, you should consider getting one."

"Yes, today is Myra's last day," Randy mumbled and rubbed his neck.

That was the problem; his search for a personal assistant just took a strange, weird turn.

Sky had called him and suggested that Addi wanted the job. Why? Why would Addi want to work for him? It was a crazy idea. The last he heard she was preparing to get married to some mega church pastor. *Was that over?*

And why did the thought of her being single make him happy?

Selena's cell phone rang, and she got up from the table.

"Hold that thought, whatever it is, I want to know what has you so distracted and I need some names."

She went to answer the phone and Randy closed his eyes.

Selena did not want to hear his current thoughts because he was thinking of offering Addi the job.

Addison Porter, who told him ten years ago that they had been lovers in another time. Addison Porter who fascinated him unduly, who he was undeniably attracted to, who he was drawn to on a level that was inexplicable to himself.

His feelings for her could easily get out of control. He

couldn't hire her as his personal assistant. It would be playing with fire. Their time to get together was two years ago, and Addi had soundly rejected him.

She had chosen someone else. He had dealt with that and moved on. He had a good thing going with Selena. He would be a fool to jeopardize it. Selena was perfect for him; she was independent, educated and a go-getter just like him.

She was a realtor with her own company and had brokered many a deal on his behalf. She was the one who had arranged for him to get his newest business, Royalty Insurance, at a very reasonable price because she thought it would be a good fit for him.

Selena was business savvy, and she probably knew him better than he knew himself because he had not been thinking about acquiring an insurance company.

They were so compatible in how driven they were that it was sometimes scary. Sometimes, he wished though that there was more of a spark, maybe a bit of the uncontrolled longing that he felt when he was around Addi.

One could not have everything perfectly; he chastised himself. He was getting married in April, a mere four months away and he was going to help plan his engagement party with Selena, and he would concentrate on the task because it was his party too.

"That was Errol." Selena came back to the table and put down the phone. "He got us a sale."

"Huge client. He is downstairs, he is coming up to celebrate, and I need to see the contracts to make sure that everything is ok. I can't believe he got the deal. Business has been good lately, like really good. This year is shaping up to be the perfect year for us."

"That's great." Randy yawned and then stood up. "I should leave you guys to your celebrations. I am feeling beat."

"Wait." Selena eyed him suspiciously. "Why were you so distracted?"

Randy considered blowing her off. Then he sighed. "I got a call today from Josh's cousin, Skyler Jefferson. Josh's sister Addi needs a job."

"Josh?" Selena asked. "Your best friend, Josh?"

"Yes." Randy nodded. "That Josh."

"His sister needs a job?" Selena asked impatiently.

"Yes," Randy nodded again, "but I don't think..."

"Hire her." Selena shrugged. "If she is even remotely capable of helping you out she would be an asset, case closed. A little cronyism never hurt anyone. She's practically family, isn't she?"

"But," Randy shook his head, "you don't understand she is..."

"Josh's little sister and you are afraid that if she sucks at the job you'll have to fire her?" Selena laughed. "Don't worry about it. I am sure that she won't cry for long. She has so many connections. Why didn't Skyler arrange to get her a job at one of the Jefferson companies?"

"Selena, she is not a little girl or a teenager, she is twenty-five and..."

The doorbell rang. Selena got up and pointed at him. "Hire her Randy. You need an assistant, stop being so picky. Since you acquired Royalty Insurance, you have hired managers and department heads, but a personal assistant is elusive. This boggles the mind."

She went to answer the door. Randy's protest was lost as Errol walked in with a big cheesy grin on his face and handed Selena a folder with what he assumed were the successfully signed contracts.

"Got it! We had the best pitch."

"Yay!" Selena started jumping around and waving the

papers in her hand.

Randy watched her indulgently for a while and then got up. "I am going home. Congrats Errol."

Errol nodded, his glasses catching the light and making him appear owlish. "Thanks."

He was a big fellow with a huge midsection that made him look permanently pregnant, and he sported a double chin. He was Selena's right-hand man, her business partner and Randy suspected that Errol was in love with her.

He would do anything for Selena. If Selena said jump off a building, he would do it without questions.

That was the kind of man she deserved, and he was not that man. The thought caught Randy unaware as he headed toward the bank of elevators in her building. He didn't love Selena, the way that Errol did, if he had, he would have married her already, and he wouldn't be apprehensive about hiring Addi.

If he loved Selena, Addi would have no power over him. As it was, he was wary of Addi on two counts.

One, she told him that they had been lovers for twenty years in another time. That was some staying power. Some people didn't even stay married for that long.

And two, he didn't want a repeat of the other timeline. He didn't want to be married to one woman and seeing another. That was just wrong and not something he would ever want to do. He had seen how his father's philandering had affected his mother.

He sat in his car for five full minutes before he picked up the phone and called Skyler. He had promised her an answer by the end of the day.

"Hey Sky," he said when she answered, "I am calling back about Addi."

"Yes." Sky sounded eager.

He was going to disappoint her.

"Why does Addi want to work for me? I thought she was going to get married or something." His curiosity got the best of him; he needed to find out what was going on with Addi.

Sky sighed. "Addi has been caught up in a string of unfortunate events, you heard about the pastor who was working with the mafia?"

"No." Randy frowned. "All I hear about New York now is 9/11 and the aftermath. What about the pastor?"

"He was Addi's fiancé. The feds busted him, and the mafia goons decided that they would take out some of their frustration on Addi."

Randy gasped. "Say what? Is she okay?"

"Yup," Sky sniffed, "she is still healing but she is returning to Jamaica for a while, and she didn't want to depend on family for help. She said she didn't want to feel like a charity case, so I thought of you. You said you were head hunting for a personal assistant and you are not family."

Randy sighed. "Sky this is not ideal."

"You don't have to hire her. Interview her at least," Sky urged him, "for old times sake. Please. I hate seeing her so despondent. Besides, I can guarantee you that Addi is a hundred times more efficient than Emma. I am so sorry about that."

Randy gripped the phone tighter. He should have just said no. But he had asked about her background story, and a tiny part of him was intrigued by this new development in Addi's life. How had she made such a blunder?

Now he had to at least interview her and maybe see her one last time. Maybe he was hyping up Addi in his mind unnecessarily. Maybe he wouldn't even be attracted to her anymore. This was 2002, eighteen months since his last encounter with her. Some of her allure would certainly be lost.

"Fine," he said to Sky. "My assistant Myra shortlisted some candidates for me to see next Monday at 10. She can come by at 1. We can have a working lunch or something."

Sky laughed. "Thank you. You could sound happier about it. You know that this is a great opportunity for you to get acquainted with her again."

"I am engaged to be married," Randy growled. "I don't want to get acquainted with Addi again."

"You'll manage just fine," Sky muttered. "I have to go, Randy. Thanks again for considering her. It means a lot to me."

She hung up before he could ask her why she was so confident that he could manage just fine.

Chapter Four

Addi drove up to Royalty Insurance Limited and was directed by a security guard at the front to the lone empty spot in the large parking lot under a sign that said, visitors. She looked at her watch and inhaled raggedly. She was too early, but she hadn't been able to relax since she got up this morning. The guesthouse where she was staying had a noisy group of revelers staying on both sides of her room, and they had a meeting right near her window about what they were eating for breakfast.

Of course, she hadn't been able to fall asleep after their discussion. She had lain awake thinking about this interview, running it over and over in her head and imagining all sorts of horrifying scenarios:

Randy laughing at her for rejecting him when he had been such a good catch;

Randy asking her how she was a resetter and her life ended up so crappy?

Addi pulled down the mirror from the sunshade flap and looked at herself assessingly. She had taken care with her makeup and had her long hair in a slicked back bun, not even a tendril of a curl out of place. Her navy suit and stark white blouse gave her a professional air. She looked the part, at least he couldn't fault her for that.

She glanced at her watch again; she was half an hour early. Maybe she should wait inside, instead of out in the car, the AC for her father's Toyota was temperamental. She got out and inhaled and headed to the gray and blue painted three-story building.

She was greeted by a receptionist at the front desk and was told that Mr. Vassell was expecting her in a few minutes. She sat and waited picking up one of the brochures to familiarize herself with the company's offerings and occasionally looking at the people who filed past her. If the walking traffic was anything to go by, Royalty Insurance was doing brisk business.

She learned that Royalty was a medium sized general insurance company previously owned by Cassius Green, who was now deceased. Randall Vassell acquired his company. All of the company's services were kept after the acquisition. They insured everything.

She put down the brochure after reading through the different coverages and closed her eyes. What was she doing here?

She didn't have to be here. She could be at home in Mandeville, working with her mother in the newly expanded hardware store or even with her dad and Uncle Stan. They had moved the construction business from the home to the town area and had expanded their services.

She could even work with Myrna Jones, her former next-door neighbor. Myrna had a thriving design business, and her husband had a complimentary upholstery business. She had helped them to be where they were now, and they were grateful. Maybe she could get a front desk job or something.

She had been Myrna's first customer. She smiled at the memory. Fresh from her reset she had been determined to get to know her neighbors and she had succeeded with the Jones'. She still kept in touch with Myrna.

She had actually done it. Changed their lives. So why was hers in such disarray?

"Mr. Vassell will see you now." The receptionist looked across at her with a smile. "He is on the third floor. His office is at the end of the corridor."

Addi got up and nodded. She felt a little nervous. Well, a lot, if she was going to be honest. She hadn't seen Randy in two years, and the last time she had turned him down. Should she call him Mr. Vassell now? Or Randall? Or plain old Randy?

She followed the directions to his office. The place was recently painted; she could smell faint whiffs of it.

She passed several offices with glass panels. Everyone seemed to be busy, some of them looked like they were with clients. She headed to the very end of the passageway with a bigger office. Randy was sitting at his desk.

She could see him through the glass. He was on the phone. She paused and drank him in. How was it possible that he looked better every time she saw him?

He was handsome on a scale of his own, low cut hair, neatly trimmed beard, eyes that were so deep brown they looked black, the whitest teeth, skin like dark chocolate.

She hadn't realized that she was just standing in the passageway ogling Randy until he made eye contact with her.

At first, he didn't react. He just looked at her. Their eyes met and tangled, and then he was the one who broke the eye contact. He put down the phone and then got up and opened the door for her.

Addi didn't move immediately because she knew this was not going to work. Randy didn't say a word as he stood at the door. It was as if they were thinking the same thing.

"Addi," Randy said huskily, "come on in."

She still dithered and then inhaled. Letting her breath out slowly. She made her feet move one in front of the other as she headed to where he stood.

"Hello, Mr. Vassell." Her voice quivered. She hoped that he didn't pick that up.

"Mr. Vassell?" Randy raised an eyebrow and then closed the door and indicated to the chair in front of his wide desk.

He sat down and then looked at her and shook his head. "Sky told me that you were battered and bruised and all of that stuff. I expected you to not look quite so good."

Addi gave a rueful shrug. "Sky and her big mouth. She shouldn't have said that!"

"I asked." Randy leaned forward in his chair. "I needed to know why my favorite time traveler who has traversed these paths before ended up here."

Addi sighed. "I ask myself the same question every day. No answers seem readily available."

"Everybody else seems to have benefited from your foreknowledge, including me." Randy laughed. "Especially me. I made a killing in the stock market. I rode the tech bubble and hopped off last year as you said, and I got property you said would be hot in the future."

"But this insurance company," Addi looked around, "I had nothing to do with this."

Randy nodded. "That's true, Cassius Green, the previous owner, died unexpectedly last year. He was just fifty. He died intestate. No will. No heirs. The business is profitable and was going for less than market value. My real estate agent told me about it, so I snapped it up before other investors heard about it."

"A good business move." Addi nodded. "I haven't been making any of those lately."

Randy propped his hand under his chin and gazed at her longer than was comfortable. "Why did you give up modeling?"

"Because it was time and I was dating a pretty conservative guy." She almost cringed when she said that.

Randy narrowed his eyes. "So he had a problem with modeling and not money laundering?"

"Something like that." Addi crossed and uncrossed her legs nervously. "The money laundering thing came as a surprise."

Randy sat back in his chair and drummed the desk. "And this was the guy you chose over me, two years ago?"

Addi swallowed. "I had my reasons."

"Your reasons were messed up. It defied logic." He glared at her.

Addi felt like clutching her handbag close to her and running from the office. Randy couldn't be making it any more transparent how he felt.

"The job itself is not something that you can't handle," Randy finally spoke again, his voice was brusque as if he meant business. The personal trivialities were over.

"This office will be my base now for the next couple of months, but I am not planning to be tied down here. I will find a general manager soon. I have various business interests. Maybe it is time I look into having an office space of my own. I don't want business to consume me though; I want to be very present at home with my wife and hands-on with my children when I get them..."

Addi tried hard not to flinch. Instead, she faked a pleasantness she just wasn't feeling. "I heard you were engaged, congratulations."

Randy didn't react. He continued speaking as if she hadn't said a thing.

"I guess what I am trying to say here, Addi is that I need a personal assistant. Emphasis on personal, you'll be doing stuff for me, like picking up my dry cleaning, taking notes in a meeting, arranging travel, planning parties, sending flowers to my fiancée. You would be doing the things that I may not be able to do; you would, in essence, be my right arm."

Addi swallowed. *Send his fiancée flowers* was ringing in her ears. She hadn't heard anything much after that.

"Do you honestly think we can work together, Addi?" Randy asked after a short period of loaded silence.

Addi dragged her eyes to his face and tried to figure out if she was a glutton for punishment.

This man, this gorgeous specimen of a man was a detriment to her peace of mind. This was mental and emotional suicide.

She was setting herself up to get hurt. Where was her sense of self-worth? She shouldn't be working for Randy and being so involved in his life and no, she didn't honestly think they could work together.

His phone rang as he waited for her to respond and she sat there woodenly as he answered the call.

He hung up the phone and sighed. "I forgot that I have an investors meeting in twenty minutes."

Addi gave him a half smile. "Seems like you need a personal assistant."

"Yep." Randy looked at her skeptically. "You never answered my question."

"Because I don't know." Addi cleared her throat. "I think we can work together. I can be professional."

"And our history, in the other time..." Randy asked, "that won't be an issue?"

"It shouldn't be," Addi squeaked, her voice coming out breathlessly. "We are different people now, and I don't remember anything about that timeline."

"Except for what you wrote down in a book and you still hold me to?" Randy reminded her not so gently.

"Well yes, I wrote stuff down. It only made sense if I didn't want to make the same mistakes twice." Addi nodded. "Besides, you are getting married soon; you've obviously moved on from the idea of us getting together..."

"Right." Randy nodded. "Well then, the job is yours if you want it. We work from this office most of the time. Your office is next door; you are going to have to get a laptop and other necessities. I will arrange for a company credit card for you. I have a meeting at the Palm Hotel; you can come along and observe. The architect is finished with the plan so it should be interesting."

He got up, and Addi looked at him unblinkingly.

"You are going to have to move faster than that," Randy said glancing at her. "Palm Hotel is across town. On our way back I show you my apartment the building is new. I started it in late 2000. It was finished five months ago. Most of the units are sold out. Except a few I reserved. One of them, a studio on the ground floor can be yours. You'll have to furnish it. I have not gotten around to those finer details yet. We'll discuss your salary in the car and also the schedule for the next couple of months."

Addi stood up hurriedly. "Yes, sir."

Randy looked at her dispassionately. "I can't deal with you calling me sir."

"Okay," Addi nodded stiffly, "Randall... Mr. Vassell when we are in company."

Randy chuckled. "I am going to have to call Josh and tell him that his little sister is calling me Mr. Vassell."

Addi rolled her eyes. "Please don't tell Josh anything about me. I don't want him worried and fretting, that's why I chose to work for you. I can't stand the family fuss."

"Okay," Randy nodded, "fair enough."

****

They were driving to the Palm Tree Hotel before it occurred to Randy that he had just offered Addi a job. He was a glutton for punishment, but he had taken one look at her walking uncertainly into the passageway this morning, and he had known that he wouldn't say no to her working for him.

It was Addison Porter. Josh's little sister. His secret fascination. The one woman who he could never completely shake from his mind. And here she was sitting in his car, looking for all the world like some exotic mock secretary in her tailored clothes and her hair clipped back in what was supposed to be a severe style but really just emphasized her cheekbones and her generous lips.

Good Lord, why was this happening to him? How was he going to do this? He abhorred the thought of being unfaithful, and he wasn't going to be. Selena deserved better.

He wondered what he had told himself in the other timeline that had enabled him to cheat on his wife of twenty years?

His attraction to Addi now was strictly physical; he could overcome it. He wasn't a base animal that operated on instinct, he had a brain, and he was going to use it. He would not succumb to it, this was a different time, and he was determined to be a better person.

He gave himself a mental nod and glanced at Addi. She had no power over him now, and that was how it would stay.

"What is this meeting about?" Addi met his gaze. Why hadn't he realized before that her eyes were the same shade of his favorite chocolate bar?

He groaned mentally. So maybe he was going to take baby steps where she was concerned, build up an immunity to her.

The meeting, he dragged his mind from his little attraction conundrum and then focused on business.

"It's an investor meeting with the major stakeholders of a resort village we are planning just a little on the outskirts of Montego Bay."

Addi whistled. "You really have a diversity of interests."

"Yes." Randy nodded. "You'll be up close and personal with them in no time. You might meet Selena there. She is an investor too."

Addi nodded and then gazed out the window away from him. He wondered what she was thinking and then castigated himself for caring. Addi's thoughts about Selena were no business of his.

But he couldn't help himself; he had to find out something. "In the other timeline who was I married to?"

Addi looked at him. "I never did tell you her name did I?"

"No, you didn't," Randy smirked. "Is it Selena by any chance? Her father is a minister too, are we on a collision course to repeating history?"

"No." Addi shook her head. "First of all, you married the daughter of Reverend P.N. St. Claire in the other timeline because he wanted somebody to take over his church. You were about to do your MBA, and he convinced you to do ministry instead and being the ambitious, driven guy that you are you took his advice. You did ministry. You married his daughter to cement your place in the family."

Randy whistled. "Wow. I see the reverend on television all the time. His daughter sings on the program."

"Yes, that's her. She sings beautifully. Her name is Kenya. She is married to her father's junior pastor. It looks like that is just her life. Marry the man who succeeds her father."

"Goodness." Randy slowed to a crawl at the traffic light. "Life is so funny, just one decision and you can have a different future. I never met Kenya. I never met the reverend St Claire; I did my final year of university in Florida. My dad sent for me, and I got to know him a little better."

"I know." Addi nodded. "Josh told me."

"I wanted to tell you personally." Randy accused her gently. "You said that we could keep in touch, but you never followed up on that."

"I know. I had other plans for my life." Addi sighed. "I didn't want to repeat the last time...I just wanted...a change. It would be foolish of me to pursue a relationship with the same guy that I did before when that relationship hadn't been ideal."

"I understand that," Randy nodded, "but what if this time around had been our chance to get it right? What if this time we got married, had children together..."

"Then I would have blown it because you are on the verge of committing to someone else," Addi said wryly, "but that's the thing about life, people make mistakes, and they live with it."

Randy grinned. "Said the former resetter who traveled back in her lifetime to change her family's lives...and mine."

"Maybe I shouldn't have interfered with yours," Addi muttered, "who knows who has a crappy life now because of me. You were a good minister you must have touched some lives."

"And I may have ruined some." Randy shrugged. "You never know, huh?"

He turned into the hotel entrance, spoke to the security and then drove toward the parking lot that was indicated. Randy turned off the vehicle and turned to Addi. "Ready to go?"

"Yes." Addi exhaled raggedly, she was feeling like a knot, all tied up inside.

"Sorry about lunch, we'll eat after this is done," Randy promised, "and then we can talk some more."

Chapter Five

The investor meeting was in a large conference room. At first, it seemed as if there were tons of people in there but looking around Addi counted thirty-five persons. They all seemed to know each other.

Randy was pulled into a conversation as soon as he hit the door. Addi could see him huddled in a group with some men who looked like they were talking intently about something.

Addi felt superfluous to requirements. Randy didn't need an assistant now. She was just there to observe so she took up residence at the back of the room where there was a buffet line of all the imaginable lunch items one could think of.

She hadn't realized that she was famished until the scent of the food hit her, and she did indulge. She picked up her plate and went from station to station. She had to sample a little bit of everything. There were several tables at the back, and she took a seat at one of them. If this was her first assignment as Randy's assistant, it wasn't going too badly at all.

"May I join you, madam?"

Addi looked up; the voice didn't match the man.

He had one of those radio disc jockey voices, fluid with the right hint of husk. He was huge not just fat. His stomach was so protruded she had doubts he could comfortably sit at the table.

"Yes, sure." Addi nodded and looked back down at her plate she didn't want to stare.

He placed his plate on the table and settled himself in the chair nearest to her. He had to push the chair out quite a bit.

"My name is Errol Daniels."

She looked over at him, "Addison Porter."

"And you came in with Randall Vassell?" Errol smiled. "I was watching from the sidelines, are you his new assistant?"

"Yes." Addi smiled at him. "It hasn't been an hour."

Errol stared at her. "You are pretty."

"Thank you." Addi smiled again.

Errol chuckled. "I don't think Selena will be pleased with just how pretty you are. You could model."

"I used to model." Addi latched on to the other part of his statement. "You know Selena?"

"Yes." Errol unfolded his utensils and then looked over at her. "I know her very well. I am her business partner and regular doormat. If you work for Randy, I guess you will see a lot of me, since they are engaged."

"Yes, I heard." Addi was curious about Errol now, more than curious. She wanted to ask him a million and one questions about Selena.

Errol looked as if he read her mind. "She's over there."

He pointed to a tall woman who had her back turned to them. She was listening attentively while the man who was speaking to her was gesticulating to demonstrate a point.

"And the man she is talking to is her brother. I have no idea why he is even here."

"I guess I'll meet her later," Addi said disappointed that she couldn't see Selena, the woman that Randy loved enough to want to marry.

Errol grunted. "In some respects, they make a good match; they are both driven, ambitious, and attractive. They are visually perfect together," Errol said the last bit grudgingly.

Addi glanced at him. "You don't sound as if you are pleased about it."

"No." Errol cut a slice of meat and chewed slowly and methodically.

Addi waited impatiently for him to elaborate.

"Why?" She asked when it looked as if Errol was going to be chewing forever.

"Oh, sorry," Errol said after he swallowed. "New weight loss gimmick, masticate your food thoroughly. My doctor said I should do it."

Addi nodded. "Is it working?"

"No." Errol shook his head. "I'll scarf this down when I get tired of the slow chewing."

"Why don't you think Selena and Randy are the perfect match?" Addi asked before Errol could put another piece of meat into his mouth.

Errol looked at her and frowned. "You called him Randy with such familiarity. Quite unusual for an employee of a few minutes."

"He is a family friend. He's best friends with my brother." Addi shrugged. "It is going to be hard to call him Mr. Vassell or Randall."

"I'd say." Errol changed the subject. "So where are you living? If you don't mind me prying, I am a realtor. I know of the best rentals around here. I know of a little bungalow that would fit you perfectly. You and that house were meant to be together."

He fished in his pocket and handed her a business card.

Addi took it and laughed. "Currently I am staying at a hotel, but Randy said something about a new building and an apartment he had there for his assistant?"

"The Primrose, lovely place. I live there, bought an apartment there as soon as it was done. I sold that property to Randy in July 2000. It was the perfect timing. I met him at a Chamber of Commerce mixer here in Montego Bay that Selena was too busy to attend. I always get the leftover events."

Addi glanced at his bitter expression and concluded that all was not well with Selena and her business partner.

"I took one look at Randy, and I knew he was ripe for a sale," Errol continued, "and I moved in for the sale. The Primrose property was just waiting for the right developer.

"I said to Randy, it is twelve acres, a developer's dream. He looked at me contemplatively and shrugged.

"For the price, I'll take it. I might do something with it. I need to be distracted. I think I am heartbroken. I was recently rejected by a fickle female who can't see sense."

Addi inhaled sharply. "Really, he said that?"

Errol nodded. "Yes, I was surprised too, guys who looked like Randy are not heartbroken. They break hearts. Unfortunately, I reported that piece of info to Selena who took over the sale after she saw him, by December they were inseparable. Apparently, I'm quite the matchmaker."

Addi stifled a gasp, July 2000 was Sky's wedding, she was the fickle female that turned down Randy. She was the one ultimately responsible for him and Selena being together. She didn't say that to Errol though.

Errol did not scarf down the food as he said he would. He ate at a measured pace. He had all kinds of tidbits to offer about the other investors.

When the meeting finally got underway, he didn't leave the table to join the others as she thought he would.

He stayed with her, offering information about everyone as it related to which property or housing would be perfect for them.

Errol, it seemed lived and breathed real estate.

"That's Mark Richards," he said pointing out one investor. "He is a two-story plantation style kind of house guy. His would have to have a big landscaped backyard, and a view. Instead, he lives in a condo. He doesn't understand what a splendid opportunity he is wasting, but the wife loves her condo and her little parties with her girlfriends in Miami. He never sees her; the secretary is looking more and more attractive.

"One day he'll up and leave her and move to the countryside. I see it on him; the condo is wearing him down."

Addi chuckled and shook her head. "Maybe you are the one wearing him down?"

"That too," Errol said quite nonplussed. "I check in on him every other month or so. The property in question is still up for grabs. It needs a particular owner. It could be a Mark Richards or a Randall Vassell."

"You see Randy as a plantation style house kind of guy?"

"Yes, Randy would be perfect for the house too. Selena on the other hand, not so much, she is kind of like Mark Richards' wife, a condo girl. No pets. No kids. No garden to look after. Always traveling for work."

"You make them sound incompatible," Addi said after a while.

"Right." Errol nodded. "Randy is going to be husband number three. He knows what he is letting himself in for."

"I didn't know she was married before." Addi widened her

eyes in consternation.

"Twice before," Errol murmured. "She doesn't talk about the first one. I guess it didn't count."

"Really?" Addi's curiosity was in overdrive. "What happened?"

Errol shut down. He looked at Addi and then looked away again. "I already said too much. I seem to be too comfortable with you, Miss Porter. It can be a good thing and a bad thing but no more dishing on Selena at least not today."

Addi raised an eyebrow. "When?"

Errol chuckled. "When you tell me stuff about Randy."

"What makes you think I know anything about Randy?" Addi frowned.

"You know, stuff like..." Errol coughed. "You are the fickle female that can't see sense, you broke his heart two years ago, and I am dying to know why you work for him now."

Addi opened her mouth. "You know?"

"Yep. I do." Errol shrugged, "I may have left out a teeny bit of information about the day I met him. He was staring at a picture of you when I came upon him in the far corner of the patio. You were posing at what looked like a gazebo."

"Yes." Addi finally got control of her mouth.

"I'd recognize you anywhere." Errol chuckled, "I told him that you were pretty and asked if I could see you. He said sure, this is the girl that got away and then he handed me your picture."

Addi swallowed. "Randy and I are complicated. You wouldn't understand."

"Just like Selena and I are complicated." Errol shrugged. "But I am sure we'll have hours of conversation unraveling our complications with the engaged couple won't we?"

"I doubt that." Addi shook her head. "I am just Randy's assistant now, and I am not getting involved with his love life."

Errol looked at her and then he started to laugh, attracting the attention of the persons who were closest to the back.

"Whatever, makes you fall asleep at night," he finally said after his uproar. He wiped his eyes. "But I will allow a change of topic for now as we are attracting a bit of attention."

****

After the meeting, Randy found her and Errol at the back of the conference room. He glanced at them suspiciously before he spoke.

"Hello, Errol. I see you met Addison."

"Yes, I did," Errol nodded, "from the moment I saw her. I said this lady looks familiar."

"I can't imagine why." Randy turned to Addi before Errol could say anything more, "I wanted you to meet Selena. She is around here somewhere."

"Behind you," Errol said placing his arms over his ample stomach and looking for all the world like an entertained Buddha.

Addi looked behind Randy, and her eyes met Selena's.

She looked older than Addi had expected, maybe thirty-five or so. She was attractive. Not cute or pretty. High forehead, brown hair, thin lips, Addi cataloged her features quickly. She was dressed impeccably and looked a little intimidating like she was used to commanding people around.

Selena tapped Randy on the shoulders, and he spun around.

"Hi, I wanted you to meet Addison Porter, my new assistant."

"Oh yes," Selena held out her hand to Addi, "I am pleased to meet you."

She shook Addi's hand firmly and then raised a brow at

Errol. "I thought you were going to the open house at three?"

She glanced at her watch. "It's now two-thirty."

"And that's why I'll get right on it." Errol got up from the table unhurriedly. "Nice to meet you, Addi. I am sure if you are going to be living at the Primrose we'll see much more of each other."

"Sure." Addi nodded.

Selena looked between Errol and Addi a frown on her face. "He is not bothering you is he, Addi?"

"No, not at all. He is fun," Addi said smiling. "And really sweet. I like Errol."

Randy and Selena looked at her incredulously.

"Well then," Selena cleared her throat, "I'll see you around too. I hope you do a fabulous job for my almost hubby."

Addi nodded. "I am up to it."

"That's what I like to hear." Selena turned to Randy. "I must go, I will call you tonight, babe. Maybe, come over? We'll talk."

She kissed him on the lips possessively and then she strode briskly out to the reception area.

"She's... er...busy," Addi said when they headed to Randy's car.

"High octane," Randy answered absently. "She reads contracts for fun."

Addi smiled. "Errol said as much. You are the same—driven, ambitious, always busy..."

"I saw you guys in deep conversation every time I turned around." Randy stopped at the car door. "What had you so engrossed?"

Addi got into the car and laughed. "Errol is simply delightful. He was describing the best properties to match people in the room."

"Yep. Sounds like him." Randy got in the car. "What did

he say was yours?"

"A bungalow." Addi chuckled. "Apparently, he has one up for rent."

"I see." Randy glanced at her. "Did he say anything about how he and I met?"

Addi nodded. "He did. He was the one who introduced you to the site where you built Primrose."

"That's all?" Randy asked heavily.

"And he said that he introduced you to Selena."

Randy exhaled noisily. "Yes, he did."

She didn't tell Randy about what Errol had said about the picture and him being sad over her rejection. He looked like he didn't want her to know and she definitely didn't want to bring it up again.

She focused on the road instead, looking away from Randy.

He didn't seem to be in the mood for conversation either. He turned on the radio to a popular afternoon show, and they listened to it in silence until they reached The Primrose.

****

The Primrose entrance didn't look very different from the entrance to the Palm Hotels where they just left, Addi thought looking around at the impeccable landscaping and the rock garden at the front. The place was larger than she had imagined it would be.

The complex was made up of three-story buildings. Each building had its own courtyard and separated by a green area. They were all painted in different colors: orange, green, blue, yellow, red, purple and lavender

"It works," Addi said out loud. "It should clash, but the colors work. Maybe it is the white trimmings on the building and the design."

Randy nodded. "It does work; the designers said that they

were the colors of the primrose plant."

"I didn't know that this complex would be so...complex," Randy shrugged, "but it made sense to use up the land and to take advantage of the view."

Addi counted eight buildings in total, one of them was a recreation area where there was a pool and a gym and a garden area, which not surprisingly had primrose planted along the edges. Randy stopped at the very last building. It was painted in hunter green.

"This is where my place is." He got out of the car and came around to her side. "I am on the top floor, the apartment where you'll be staying is on the ground floor. Let me first show you around and then we go up to mine."

Addi nodded. "Yes sure."

There were eight one-bedroom apartments on the ground floor, each had its own little garden at the back and was screened by a privacy fence.

The one that Randy showed her at the end of the building was empty. It was spacious too, and she was mentally decorating it before Randy intruded on her thoughts.

"It is going to rain."

"Huh?" Addi looked at him blankly.

"It's overcast." Randy pointed out giving her a half smile. "You like this kind of thing don't you, decorating and stuff, I can practically see you salivating over there."

"Yes." Addi nodded. "I do like it."

"I remember when Josh and I helped you to paint your bedroom and you had us clear out that music room. You were in your element."

"I was, maybe that's my calling." Addi indicated to the open plan living room and kitchen. "The place is nice."

"Thanks." Randy leaned on the wall and looked at her lazily. "Do you want to decorate it alone or should I ask an interior decorator to help out?"

"I'll do it," Addi said. "It's no trouble at all. It's a modest space."

"You can take the rest of the week to do it," Randy said. "Sorry I didn't get this done before. You could have just moved in then."

"It's no problem." Addi spun around. "I am cool with it, and I am cheaper than an interior decorator."

Randy pulled the patio door closed. "Okay then. Let's go up to my place."

Addi followed him sedately. They took the elevator up to the third floor. There were just four apartments on that floor.

"All of them three bedrooms," Randy said opening the door to his. It was laid out like the one bedroom, just on a grander scale, there was a view of the sea in the distance, a cruise ship was making its way to the harbor and so was the rain.

"So this is where I live," Randy said briskly. "My bedroom is through there. My office here. He was opening doors and moving fast. Addi could barely keep up.

"Some mornings we'll work here instead of the office." Randy went back to the living room and sat down. Addi sat across from him.

The decor was lovely, and it fit Randy. It had muted earth-toned colors with a pop of color here and there.

She looked around and then at him.

Randy seemed as if he was in deep thought. He was staring at the patio where the rain was coming down in sheets.

Addi sat there and held herself still. She felt so wound up and skittish around Randy. If he said boo now she would probably fly up out of the seat and shout guilty.

Yes, I am guilty!

I wanted to be back in your life. Who was I fooling? And

I am not happy that you are engaged to Selena! I messed up badly by holding out for some new relationship that was a huge mistake.

Randy looked at her as soon as the thought entered her head and she averted his eyes.

"Shyness in Addi, we can't have that," Randy murmured. "Not one bit."

Addi looked at him after that and struggled to hold his gaze. The tension and awareness in the air was palpable.

"No, we can't have it." She swallowed and straightened in the seat. "That was just a lapse."

Randy shook his head. "You know what this is? This is crazy. It is pretense; we are very aware of each other. You feel it. I feel it. Let us not pretend that it's not there."

Addi croaked. "Okay."

"Good." Randy inhaled. "Maybe that is the first step to killing whatever crazy chemical madness has us in its clutch."

"Yes." Addi nodded.

"I was fine with myself before you came along." Randy gritted out. "I was going to marry Selena, we'll be happy. It is still going to happen."

"Sure." Addi blinked back tears. "Yes. I er...I completely understand."

Chapter Six

"That girl Addi is gorgeous," Errol said to Selena as soon as he lumbered into the office on Friday. "Did you know that she is living in the same building as your fiancé?"

"Yes." Selena bit out. She had a pile of papers in front of her, and she was watching an infomercial about the company that she had commissioned an advertising company to do.

"Aren't you the least bit jealous that Randy has a stunner working for him?" Errol decided to needle her, "a younger, sweeter, prettier, nicer girl than you?"

Selena looked up at Errol. "What's your point, snake?"

"Nothing, just an observance." Errol parked himself in one of the sofas in her office. His newest diet and exercise program was a stunning failure. He felt out of breath, and he had only walked from the car to Selena's office, which couldn't be more than fifty steps.

"I have never been insecure," Selena looked at Errol dispassionately, "Randy loves me. It would be pointless to be jealous of a girl that is quite clearly a pity hire. His best friend's sister. Have you seen Josh? The guy is stunning; obviously, I knew his sister would also be pretty. Besides, Joe says she has issues. Randy would be wise not to touch her with a bargepole."

"Joe Burns, your brother?" Errol raised an eyebrow. "What kind of issues, does he say this girl has?"

Selena sighed. "I am not into gossiping."

"You?" Errol chuckled and then wiggled his finger at Selena. "Randy likes her, and I am not sure that I would be so confident about his so-called love. You can't dismiss this girl, Addi, so easily."

"Here we go again," Selena sighed. "You are a jealous toad. You have been trying to break up Randy and me since the beginning. Did you close the sale at the open house?"

"Of course," Errol said confidently, "I close all my sales. I am the best real estate agent here. You would perish without me."

"That might have been true up to two years ago, but I am matching you big deal for big deal lately," Selena smirked. "Nevertheless, I am glad that this company is half yours."

"Gratitude." Errol placed his hand on his heart in a dramatic gesture. "Randy's humanity and innate kindness is rubbing off on you."

"I am grateful to you when you complete a sale, and I have expressed that to you," Selena said. "I don't know what else you want."

"Maybe I want you to stop marrying the wrong men," Errol grunted. "Two down, a third one to go."

"And marry you instead?" Selena looked at him cross-eyed. "Are you taking your meds, Errol?"

"It is not so far-fetched." Errol shrugged. "Our marriage would be perfect. We are partners in everything else."

Selena rolled her eyes. "Stop the madness."

"I gave you better orgasms than all of them." Errol grinned. "That has to count for something."

"We had a one-month thing." Selena growled, "We agreed to never speak of it again. Now leave my office."

"Not so fast." Errol's jowls jiggled as he sat up straighter in the chair. "We were on the verge of an understanding when you met Randy. You and I have more in common than you and Randy. Call off the marriage, Selena, and stop being pig-headed."

"No." Selena growled, "I love Randy."

"Why? Because he is slim and handsome and has muscles that just won't quit and when he walks into the room all the women envy you?" Errol snarled. "That is superficial, and you know that!"

"He is not just a pretty face!" Selena slapped the desk. "What is it with you? Randy has so many other qualities. He is ambitious and kind and driven and for your information not that it is any of your business, my orgasms with him are just fine."

"You are deluded," Errol growled. "I introduced you to him, and I regret it greatly. You were just on the verge of loving me when you met Randall Vassell, and since then you have been mesmerized. He is not in love with you, and you are making a mistake."

Errol struggled to get out of the settee. He glared at Selena. "You know I love you, you know I would do anything for you. You know that. Can Randy say the same? Can he, Selena?"

Selena gritted her teeth in frustration. "My engagement party is two weeks away. You are becoming unbearably annoying with this 'don't marry Randy' foolishness."

"I don't want to be husband five or six when you decide that the best thing that can happen to you is me," Errol growled. "I am running out of patience. If I didn't love you so much, I would leave now and let you come to the realization that you need me in your life!"

He walked out of the office as Selena struggled to come up with a retort. That was enough wearing down for the day. His strategy was two-fold, wear her down and get her jealous.

Initially, he had thought that Addison Porter would be an ally, she could convince Randy that he was making a mistake while he worked on Selena but he was rethinking that strategy.

Addison didn't seem to be interested in Randy. She genuinely wanted to be his assistant.

For one week he had his faithful spies reporting to him, and he was left with nothing. Wanda, the receptionist at Royalty Insurance, said he was way off; they seemed to be regular employer and employee.

Vanessa, who lived in the green building two doors from Addi, said Randy had not even visited the apartment to check on it after it was decorated. They were keeping their distance from each other.

He was in this alone.

He sat hard in his office chair. The poor thing squeaked in protest. It would probably be changed in a couple of weeks anyway.

He whisked his mind back from broken chairs and back to the matter at hand. He needed a plan.

His secretary Luna pushed her head around the door. "I have some messages."

"Later," Errol fanned her off, "I need to think."

"Okay," Luna came into the room, "but I am leaving early. I have a date."

Errol raised an eyebrow. "What flexible hours you have

my dear."

"I squared this off with you last week." Luna pouted. "My guy is visiting from Canada. I need the entire weekend."

Errol frowned. "What about the fellow you have here?"

"He thinks that he is the only man that will find me attractive, so he treats me like a discarded pair of slippers. Well, guess what, he is in for a rude awakening because I have options." Luna grinned. "I will teach him a lesson this weekend. He says he does not do jealousy, but we'll see this weekend."

"Mmmm... Interesting." Errol rubbed his chin. "Leave the messages on your desk, please."

"You should do the same with Miss Selena," Luna said before moving away. "Instead, of just sitting around and pining after her, find somebody else. You'll see how fast she comes to her senses. That woman takes you for granted too much."

Errol froze, the idea had never occurred to him. "Thanks, Luna."

"You are welcome, sir." Luna grinned. "Have a nice weekend."

"You too." Errol nodded.

And then the thought rippled through his mind, *there had only ever been one woman for him, and that was Selena. She knew it, and she took full advantage of him because of it.*

What if he turned the tables on her? Maybe, he could make her jealous of him. The thought boggled the mind. Selena had never been jealous of him. Maybe, because he had never actively tried to make her jealous.

He contemplated the thought with a small smile on his lips. It would be a nice change from their regular relationship.

He had known Selena from university; she was already married to husband number one when he met her. She had married young— shotgun style. Her ultra-conservative parents had insisted on it after she became pregnant. She had lost the baby not long after the hasty wedding.

By the time he was in a study group with Selena at university, in their sophomore year, she was going through a divorce. She was just nineteen.

He had stuck around as her friend after university. It was only natural that they would start a business together since they had so many similar interests. He had been an agent at one realtor firm, and she had been an agent at another.

They started Daniels and Burns Realtors after dinner one evening and plotted what they could do if they ran their own company. For one full year after their startup, he had mistakenly thought that he was finally being tugged out of the friend zone but then Selena introduced him to John Lee—husband number two.

He had cautioned her about marrying him, mostly out of rabid jealousy but she would not listen. She had been in love.

John had been an okay guy. They probably would have lasted, but his parents hated Selena, and they were a close family.

He couldn't count the number of evenings that he had stayed behind at the office as Selena cried on his shoulders about her in-laws and how they treated her. It was no surprise that two years later John asked for a divorce.

Selena was only glad to do it. Their relationship had soured anyway.

Just when her divorce was finalized, and she was single again, and he was completely out of the friend zone. He met Randall Vassell, and there he was again, pushed firmly back into the friend zone as if their month of intimacy in June 2000 had never happened.

It had taken a superhuman effort to still be working with

her and pretend that they hadn't been practically living together. She had told him that she loved him. And he had felt that it was genuine. She had been genuine.

Why was it that Selena always overlooked him for slimmer guys? Guys like Randall Vassell?

He spun in his chair hearing it squeak ominously under his 350-pound bulk. He had always been a chubby boy who appreciated food especially the unhealthy stuff, and he had grown into a big guy with a distinct abhorrence to what people called healthy foods. He was not made to eat like a rabbit and flagellate himself to death on some trap of death instrument in the gym.

He wasn't going to lose one hundred and fifty pounds by June either, just to show Selena that he had potential. He was who he was for now. Selena had accepted him like this once; she could do it again.

Maybe he could follow Luna's advice and take a different route, charm the pants off Addison Porter. Perhaps then he could make both Selena and Randy jealous, and then they hopefully could come to their respective senses.

Chapter Seven

"**W**hat do you think about fresh flowers for the venue?" Kathia asked Randy one week from the engagement party. Selena had sent her to him because she was on a business trip and he was supposedly available. He had just heard one of Kathia's questions. She had been sitting in the office for nearly twenty minutes, and he had completely tuned her out.

"I don't know why I came by," Kathia mumbled when he declined to answer. "This is madness, you and Selena are too busy to get married."

She jotted down something in her ledger book and then caught his eye.

"Good. You are back with me."

"I was always here," Randy said faintly, he was waiting for an important business email. He didn't have time for inconsequential things like flowers and colors and which wine glasses to use.

Why on earth had Selena insisted on an engagement party?

And why had he said yes? Knowing her, it would probably be an opportunity to do some schmoozing with prospective property purchasers. His list of invitees was less than thirty, but the invitation list was close to three hundred.

He was getting weary of the whole thing; he just wanted it over and done with. He completely missed Kathia's other question when he saw Addi collecting a huge bouquet of roses in the passageway.

She headed back to her office while reading the card. Who was sending her flowers? He got up before he realized it and then sat back down.

What was he doing? For two weeks Addi was around, and he was handling it quite fine. They could be the poster children for professionalism. They were taking great pains to avoid touching or being in a confined space too long. He was the soul of decorum. His grandmother would be proud.

But this flowers thing had his curiosity in high drive.

"What do you think about 80s music?" Kathia asked him. "Do you or Selena like it? Should we focus more on love songs or would you prefer just instrumentals?"

Randy looked at his computer; an email had just come in. He looked up at Kathia vaguely.

"Ask my PA what I like, she has a general idea."

He completely missed the sullen pout that Kathia threw his way as she stood up with her file in hand.

****

I hope you are settling well into your new job, Errol D

Addi read the note over and over again and couldn't suppress a giggle. Errol Daniels sent her gorgeous red roses. She didn't know what to make of it. She put it in the center of her desk and admired it for a brief while.

The party planner who was in Randy's office knocked on

her door and then came in, a stressed look on her face.

"Hi." She walked further into the room.

"Can you please help me? My name is Kathia, and I am planning the engagement party."

"Oh yes, the engagement party," Addi made a face. "Have a seat. What can I help you with?"

"Everything." Kathia sat down looking harassed. "I have never worked with two people quite like Randy and Selena. I have a party in a week's time, and I have no idea what to do! I can't get them to sit down for long enough to give me anything, and it is down to crunch time."

Addi looked at Kathia with pity. "I am not the right person to help."

"Randy said you knew what he liked," Kathia said stubbornly. "I need to plan something today!"

"He said that?" Addi leaned back in her chair. Over the past two weeks, she had an idea of what professional Randy liked. She was stumped as it related to anything personal. One thing that was glaringly obvious was that he didn't want this engagement party.

Was that because he didn't want to marry Selena?

She could only wish.

"The venue is the Palm Tree ballroom," Kathia said intruding on her thoughts, "Three hundred people, time: seven o'clock, live band: already booked. I have no clue what other personal touches either couple wants. I had to harass Selena for the guest list personally."

"Mmmm." Addi closed her eyes, picturing the Palm Tree ballroom. She had looked in there on the way to the conference a couple weeks ago.

If it were her engagement party, she could envision it decorated in light blue and silver, and she would have the band play Magnet and Steel, the Walter Egan version.

Magnet was Randy's nickname for her in the previous timeline according to her book.

"Fresh flowers or fake?" Kathia asked intruding on her little inappropriate reverie. "Which do you think Randy would like?"

"Fresh of course." Addi smiled. She didn't know if Randy liked fresh or not, but she did. She leaned forward and put forth her ideas about Randy's engagement party to Selena. Completely disregarding the little fact that it was not her party.

****

Randy stuck his head around Addi's door. "I have a dinner party invite from Linton Reid. He was a friend of the previous owner, Cassius Green, and is threatening to go with other insurers. I think we need to soothe his ruffled feathers; his is a pretty big account. I need you to be my plus one."

He looked at the flowers sitting on her desk curiously and then back at her. "Be ready at eight."

Addi looked up from her laptop, she had her headphones in her ears, and she had not heard a word. "Huh?"

"What CD are you listening to?" Randy folded his arms and leaned on the wall.

"70s mix." Addi took off the headphones. "By the way, that is what I told Kathia to play at your engagement party."

Randy shrugged. "I don't have any favorite music. It doesn't matter to me."

Addi gasped. "Shocking."

Randy nodded. "I know."

"You don't have any favorite music to dedicate to Selena?"

"No." Randy raised an eyebrow.

"Any little nicknames from a song?" Addi persisted.

"No." Randy scowled. "Where are you going with this?"

"Nowhere, it's nothing." Addi cleared her throat. "I told

her to use light blue and silver as your main colors."

"Sounds pretty," Randy said nonchalantly, "who sent you flowers?"

Addi looked at the vase and grinned, "Errol Daniels."

"Selena's Errol?" Randy looked surprised. "Why?"

"Maybe he is just a friendly guy." Addi smiled. "It was sweet of him."

Randy shook his head. "Errol is not sweet, and red roses are not friendly."

Addi changed the topic. "What were you saying earlier?"

Randy repeated himself and then spun around abruptly and headed to his office. He was feeling unaccountably jealous of Errol and all because he sent her flowers, how petty of him.

****

Addi left the office that evening carrying her flowers. It would look better in the apartment. Besides, Randy spent the entire day curling his lips in disdain when he saw them. She had a feeling that if she left them in the office overnight, they would meet an unfortunate end.

She had time to kill before she needed to get ready. She was letting herself into the apartment when Vanessa from two doors over came out of her apartment in gym gear.

She was a gym instructor at Muscle Up, a new gym in the town center. She was also a personal trainer who had a slew of clients she was always rushing to one appointment after the other. She had shared little titbits about herself every day for the past couple of weeks.

She was a pretty girl and extremely friendly. She reminded Addi of her cousin, Sky. They had similar facial features; same light skin, fine curly hair and they had the same ease when dealing with people. Addi had warmed to her the minute she had moved in two weeks ago. She had a feeling that they could be good friends.

"Hey," Vanessa smiled at her, "Nice flowers."

"Thanks," Addi nodded.

"Errol finally made his move." Vanessa grinned locking her door.

"You know Errol?" Addi spun around and looked at Vanessa in astonishment.

"Yep, for years. He's my best pal." Vanessa smiled. "Errol has been hounding me to spy on you to make sure that you are single. It's funny, I have never seen him this worked up about a woman before. You lucky girl you. Errol is a big guy with a big heart."

Vanessa winked at her and headed to her car.

Addi fumbled for her keys and let herself into the apartment.

Was Errol worked up about her?

Good heavens, no. She put the flowers down on the center table and sat staring at it with consternation.

Now, this was awkward. She was not even remotely attracted to Errol, and it was not because of his size.

No. She was just not into relationships. She still had the rope burns around her neck to remind her just how careful she had to be. It was too soon after the whole Devin Garcia mistake.

But if Randy had been the one to show interest... she wouldn't think twice, not now.

She tried to crush the thought.

And was happy to be distracted from it when her cell phone rang.

A new, unfamiliar number appeared on the screen. She answered cautiously.

"Hello."

"Hello." Errol chuckled. "I hope you got the flowers."

"I did." Addi clutched the phone closer to her ear and tried to relax. "Thank you. They were lovely."

"Did Randy see them?" Errol asked eagerly.

"Well, yes." Addi cleared her throat. "Errol, we need to talk about...I am just not interested. I mean I am not in the frame of mind for a relationship right now."

"That's okay." Errol sounded nonplussed. "Did Randy display any jealousy when you got the flowers?"

Addi frowned at the phone. "Huh?"

"I sent them because I wanted him jealous," Errol muttered. "Please tell me it worked."

"I don't know. Why would you want Randy to be jealous?"

"Because this sham of a marriage can't happen," Errol growled. "He had feelings for you. I want him to call off the wedding."

"Oh, heavens." Addi reached under her turtleneck blouse and rubbed her neck. "Are you seriously thinking that I have the power to somehow change Randy's mind from his imminent marriage?"

"It is worth a shot," Errol said. "Do you want us to meet and discuss the battle plan tonight?"

"I don't want to break up Randy' engagement," Addi said, exasperation creeping into her voice.

"Liar." Errol dared to laugh at her blatant lie. "You have feelings for him, just as how I have feelings for..."

"Selena," Addi whispered. It finally dawned on her that this was why Errol was insisting on the plan to break up the engagement. She had had an indication of this when they had met before, but now it was solidified.

"You love Selena?" It was a rhetorical question she didn't expect Errol to answer.

"We can meet and discuss it tonight," Errol sighed heavily, "give you my reasons."

"I can't," Addi said. "I have a dinner party to attend. It is business."

"Oh." Errol sounded disappointed. "What about tomorrow night then? There is this pretty little place called Jam Pub they serve the most divine jerk chicken."

"I can't promise that I will have any effect on Randy now," Addi said hesitantly. "We'll be wasting our time. I don't know if this is a good plan."

"Trust me, it is." Errol sounded sure of himself. "I'll pick you up. We'll talk. Have a good time. At the least, you will be a good person to get to know, and I can be a good friend."

Addi smiled when he said that.

"Okay then. Count me in. Just for the free dinner though and the outing. I haven't been anywhere casually since I have been here. It has so far been all business."

"Right, I will change that." Errol chuckled and hung up.

****

Addi was running out of outfits to hide the rope burn around her neck. She would have to start seriously thinking of wearing scarves. In the past, she only wore them in winter, and she felt that she would look odd wearing them in Jamaica where the weather didn't call for it.

The swelling where the rope had tightened around her neck had shrunken in size, but there were still blue back marks and a raw pink mark which looked worse than it felt, it stood in stark contrast to her dark skin and couldn't be covered with makeup. It had to breathe and be allowed to get better. She slumped on the bed after her shower.

She needed an outfit to wear to a business dinner. She needed something understated and simple, something that would match her purple and yellow scarf.

She settled on a yellow crochet dress that Sky had given

her for her birthday last year and her matching yellow crochet wedge heels.

She pulled back her hair into a long curly ponytail and put on sparkly butterfly earrings. And then inspected herself in the mirror. She looked presentable. She was ready to go by seven-thirty and was holding the phone wondering if she should call Randy or go up to his apartment.

Her doorbell rang, and she went to see who it was.

Randy was standing there in a dark suit, no tie, clean-shaven, smelling good. He was like a smorgasbord for the senses. She didn't know which one to focus on first and she didn't get the chance to.

"Hey," he smiled at her briefly. "You clean up well."

"Thank you...er... you too."

He looked at his watch briefly. "Let's get going. The party is at his house in the hills. It will take us a while to get there."

"Okay," Addi nodded just as briskly. As usual, she struggled for control when she was in Randy's presence. "I need to get my purse."

And some breathing space to appreciate that this hunky, mahogany man with the brown, sultry eyes was standing at her door.

But she had turned him down two years ago.

She was mad.

She stood in the living room and helplessly looked around. Mentally unstable. Crazy. Her synapses were not working.

What on earth were synapses again?

"Addi," Randy said behind her. "You are just standing there."

"Yes." Addi nodded jerkily. She had to stop admiring him so much. She had to stop feeling like a star-struck idiot when she was close to him. She thought she had this under control, but Randy in casual business attire was breathtaking.

"I like what you did with the place," Randy said looking around.

"Thanks." Addi nodded and headed to the bedroom for her purse. When she came out, Randy was outside talking on his cell phone.

He cut the call when she locked the door and then indicated to his car. "The vehicle awaits my lady."

I am not your lady! Addi felt like yelling, *and it's my fault!*

She was having time traveler's remorse. She had finally and spectacularly regretted thinking that she could rewrite her life and in the process rewrite her feelings for Randy. That wasn't happening.

Constant exposure was not a solution; neither was distance.

Unfortunately, he didn't seem as affected as she was. He had gotten over the idea of them being together. She wondered if Errol knew that trying to make Randy jealous would lead to a spectacular failure.

As soon as he started the car, the radio station that he was listening to came on. It was a news station.

Randy glanced at her. "Sorry, I have gotten boring in my old age. Want some music?"

"Sure." Addi nodded. "It would put me in a dinner party mood."

"Find a station. You have full access," Randy said. "Sorry, I have no CDs I keep forgetting to get some."

"And you don't like anything specific anyway." Addi grinned, turning the radio station until she heard the distinct voice of *Ali Campbell* from *UB 40* with one of her favorite versions of the song, *I Can't Help Falling In Love with You.*

Randy glanced at her sharply. "Trying to tell me something, Addi?"

"What? No!" Addi protested, a little bit too loudly, a little bit too guiltily. "It's just a song, that's just randomly playing on the radio!"

"Hmmpf." Randy grinned, "just playing with you."

Addi grinned back half-heartedly. "I knew that."

Except she didn't.

Chapter Eight

Linton Reid's residence was a renovated inn in the Round Hill area. The place was as charming as to be expected given the address. It was pretty close to the famous Round Hill Hotel and Villas.

Randy was suitably impressed when he drove up the winding driveway to the villa. He hardened his resolve to not lose Linton Reid as a client.

He looked over at Addi, who was looking quite spectacular tonight and grimaced. Asking her to come along had not been a brilliant idea, but she was his personal assistant.

If Selena had not gone to Kingston to clinch some huge deal, which was the highlight of her life, he would have asked her to come with him instead. Selena knew how to work a room better than anybody he knew. Before the end of the night, she would have had Linton Reid not only keeping his accounts at Royalty but also promising to buy property he didn't know he wanted.

That was just one of the benefits of having Selena at his side and as his wife. He had to enumerate the reasons to himself every day, especially since Addi was here.

"Heavy thoughts?" Addi broke into his reverie.

"Not really." Randy inhaled. "We have one thing to do now—convince this client that he should stay with the company."

"Okay." Addi nodded. "You want us to tag team him, hold him up at fork point at dinner or beg him with tears?"

Randy laughed. He couldn't help it. He had been so busy hardening his heart against Addi that he had managed to forget that she could be quite humorous when she wanted to be.

"Come on." He got out of the car and went to her side of the car and helped her out. His hand lingered on hers a little bit too long for comfort. "We'll er..." he had forgotten what he wanted to say. Addi was standing too near.

"We'll wing it," he finally said huskily closing the car door behind her and heading to the brightly lit reception room.

An elegantly dressed older woman, who could be a dead ringer for Dionne Warwick, greeted them in the reception area.

"Welcome." She smiled at Randy and then Addi. "My name is Iris Reid, Lincoln's mother. I am playing hostess this evening. Please follow me."

They followed her to a vast open space area that Randy assumed used to be the Inn's lobby. It was scattered with several seating arrangements and orchid centerpieces. Linton was holding court in the center with a small group of people. He was taller than average, maybe 6' 3, clean-shaven, in his early fifties but he didn't look it.

He greeted Randy with a firm handshake as soon as he saw him.

"Randall Vassell, good for you to join me this evening," and then he turned to Addi, "and this is?"

"Addison Porter," Addi smiled at him a tad bit too warmly for comfort. "I am Mr. Vassell's PA."

Randy didn't miss the way that Linton looked at her ring finger and the long handshake between them that was mercifully broken up by the arrival of another dinner guest.

He was almost bristling with displeasure when Addi turned to him innocently.

"This place is gorgeous. It still has the old inn feel. I haven't heard Harry Bellefonte's Banana Boat Song in a while." She was referring to the music playing in the background.

"Yes," he said abruptly and then was forced to modulate his tones. Why on earth was he so pissed?

She couldn't help being attractive, and it was unfair to think she would not attract attention especially from Linton, a man rumored to have a weakness for beautiful women.

Through most of the dinner party, Randy found himself thinking that he shouldn't have taken Addi as his plus one. Obviously, Linton found her fascinating and had her engaged in deep conversation for most of the evening, even going so far as to neglect the rest of his guests as he gave Addi his undivided attention.

Randy wondered if he had forgotten that he had invited the rest of them, a small group of fifteen or so persons. The man to his left was a doctor and quite reserved. His several attempts to engage him in conversation fell flat. Iris Reid was to his right, and he had the distinct impression that Iris was flirting with him.

It was confirmed when he felt her hands massaging his legs under the table. He had to remove it several times firmly.

"You are so handsome," Iris murmured in his ear when dessert was served, "I can't help myself from feeling if all of those muscles are real."

Randy looked at her solemnly, "I am engaged to be married. I am not on the market anymore."

Iris chuckled. "So why do you keep looking over at the girl you arrived with? Gorgeous girl by the way. She seems taken with my son. She can join you and me in bed. I am not partial to either sex if you know what I mean."

Randy grimaced. His already non-existent appetite fled.

"No thank you." He made sure that all the revulsion that he felt could spill over in his voice.

"Your loss." Iris shrugged. "It would have been a spectacular experience to remember when you are bored with the new wife."

The night couldn't end fast enough for Randy. He pleaded that he had to have an early start in the morning to release himself from Iris' clutches.

"Thanks for coming, man." Linton shook his hand vigorously. "Addi here convinced me to stay with your firm and try out the Marine Insurance coverage you guys have. I need something like that."

They were heading to the car, and Randy realized that he was seething. A vein throbbed at the side of his head, and his hand was not quite steady when he started the car.

"What's wrong?" Addi asked him softly, cautiously.

Randy gritted his teeth before answering and then realized that he was too worked up to answer. "Nothing!"

Addi squinted at him and turned fully in her seat. "I think something is wrong with you."

"Nope. I am fine." Randy growled. "Just peachy."

Addi gave him a confused frown and then turned to face the windscreen and closed her eyes.

Randy didn't trust himself to talk until they were back at the complex. He parked at her apartment and then said solemnly.

"I am not paying you to flirt with men, Addison."

"I wasn't flirting." Addi removed her seat belt in a huff. "You said we were going to a dinner party to convince Linton Reid to stay with your company. Mission accomplished. I should be getting accolades and offers of a raise, but here you are like a big, grumpy, sore bore."

"Sore bore?" Randy raised an eyebrow.

"Yes." Addi nodded. "What's wrong with you?"

"What were you and Linton talking and giggling about all evening?" Randy growled.

Addi widened her eyes. "Does it matter?"

"Yes." Randy turned to her fully. "Yes, it does. I am not running an escort service. I didn't take you to the party to use your sexual allure on the guy."

Addi sighed. "Sexual allure? You are so off the mark. We were talking about history, believe it or not. I complimented him on the decor of the place. He said he was trying to be as accurate as possible with the 1930's decor. Then he made a quip about wishing that he could time travel and I told him to be careful what he wished for because I have time traveled and I messed up my life.

"He found what I said fascinating and so I ended up telling him about resetters. I told him about being a resetter and going back in time to fifteen and how I wanted a different life this time around but..."

She bit her lip.

"But..." Randy rasped.

"But history is shaping up to repeat itself albeit a little later than before." Addi inhaled. "Randy, I shouldn't be back here in your space. We are doing it again. We are attracted again. I can feel it."

"No, we are not doing it again." Randy inhaled knowing he

was lying to himself. "I can't be that kind of man. I won't be that kind of man. This time is different. I am with a different woman. It is a different me. I'll never cheat on Selena."

"And if I tell you that I am planning to see Linton Reid?" Addi asked huskily. "How would you react?"

Randy swallowed as if he had tasted something foul. "He is a client. We don't date our clients."

"I am just a mere employee of Randy Vassell," Addi said jokingly, "I can quit."

Randy looked at her sharply. "Just to date him?"

"No." Addi shook her head, "because it is the right thing to do now. You and I are dancing around the inevitable, trying to deny this thing that is between us."

"We don't have anything between us," Randy said stubbornly.

"So why are you acting like a jealous toad," Addi hissed. "Don't deny it, that's why you were mad."

"That and the fact that Iris Reid wanted us to do a threesome." Randy sighed. "See you don't know everything."

"His mother?" Addi gasped, "are you serious!"

"Yes," Randy smiled weakly, "she sexually harassed me all throughout dinner."

"Irresistible Randy." Addi chuckled. "How did you turn her down?"

"Told her no point blank." Randy grimaced. "She handled it well. At least she stopped trying to grab my crotch under the table."

Addi laughed. "But Linton is so normal."

"I wouldn't know, I barely spoke to the man," Randy shrugged, "you monopolized him all night. You seriously considering dating him?"

Addi shook her head. "No, he is a little older than my dad, and he mentioned that he has grandchildren. I am not bashing the thirty years older thing; it's just not my cup of tea. Besides, he is a little paranoid. He said that he thinks that Cassius Green, his friend was murdered and didn't just die peacefully in his sleep. He had to meet you to see if you had something to do with it."

"Me?" Randy looked perplexed. "I never met the man. Insurance was not even in my thoughts until Selena mentioned it."

Her scarf chose that minute to unravel itself and pool on her lap. She hoped Randy couldn't see the welts on the side of her neck, but he did.

"That looks painful," he whispered.

"You weren't supposed to see them," Addi muttered, wrapping the scarf around her neck in a haphazard manner.

"If you hadn't turned me down in July 2000," Randy said harshly, "you wouldn't have gotten engaged to that guy, you wouldn't have been tied up, you wouldn't have had those scars. We would most definitely be married by now and started a family together."

Addi hung her head guiltily. "Maybe. I was pretty determined to live my life without you in it this time around."

"And how is that working out for you?" Randy growled,

"Like torture." Addi's eyes glistened with tears. "Goodnight Randy."

She opened the car door and scrambled out before he could react. He watched her as she walked to her apartment and let herself in. He watched as she turned on the living room lights and then he watched as they went off.

He was one step away from following her to the door. He was one step away from putting them both out of their torture. He imagined that he would just knock on the door and ask her to let him in and then spend the night touching her the way he wanted to. Making love to her as if there was no tomorrow... but there was Selena an engagement party in six days, and a wedding in ninety.

He closed his eyes and willed himself to gain some restraint. His phone rang just when he was about to open the car door. It was Selena.

****

"Hi Babe," Selena purred in his ear, "you are speaking to the woman who just landed the mother of all deals. Even bigger than Errol's. I hope he can live this down. We have to celebrate when I get home tomorrow."

Randy inhaled in relief.

Relief at hearing her voice.

It brought balance, stopped him from doing something stupid like banging on Addis' door and confessing that he was weak and tired of fighting.

This was Selena. His fiancée. He hadn't chosen her to be his wife lightly. It had been a levelheaded decision where he weighed the pros and cons. They were good together.

Together they could build their own dynasty, do marvelous things in business together, even though she didn't tie him up in knots emotionally; she didn't make him feel slightly off balance with her presence.

"Hey." He headed for the elevator. Passing Addis' walkway with barely a glance. "I missed you tonight. Had a dinner party at Linton Reid's house. His mother is a barracuda."

"Tell me more." Selena laughed. "Better yet, tell me tomorrow, face to face. How does Jam Pub sound? We have not been out in ages. I want to see my honey again."

Randy agreed wholeheartedly. He would welcome anything that would take his mind off Addison Porter and put it squarely back on his intended where it belonged.

Chapter Nine

Addi was not in the mood for work when she got up in the morning. She didn't want to see Randy today, and she was in no mood to go to dinner with Errol. She was in the midst of half-heartedly pulling on her favorite work pants when Sky called.

"How is it going?" Sky asked cheerfully. "You have been ridiculously tight-lipped for the past two and a half weeks. I thought you would have bagged Randy by now and the engagement party would be canceled. Instead, I got a reminder about it in my inbox. Not coming by the way."

"I knew that was your intention," Addi mumbled, "and at the time I didn't care, but it was wrong to come and work for Randy."

"You still have three months to stop the wedding." Sky was obviously not listening to a word Addi was saying.

Addi held up two blouses in front of her and put the phone on hands-free. "What blouse should I wear green or purple?

I am going on a date after work."

"Date?" Sky squealed, "with who?"

"A guy," Addi teased her cousin.

"You almost made me burn my mouth with this raspberry leaf tea," Sky muttered, "Which guy?"

"Why are you drinking raspberry leaf tea?" Addi decided on the green blouse. It was cowl necked and cute and could transition from day to night out wear. "I thought you hated teas."

"I do hate teas but my sister-in-law, Milly, the health nut, convinced me that red raspberry leaf tea was good for strengthening and toning my uterine wall. Apparently, it is supposed to make labor shorter and less painful. She did it for all three of her pregnancies, and it seemed to work, so I am doing it for mine. My doctor said it was okay and there is an abundance of the shrub behind the house in Mandeville. I had my dad send me some."

"Oh." Addi pulled on the blouse and was feeling quite pleased that she had distracted Sky from questioning her about Randy. "So how is the baby coming along?"

"Fine. Simba is quite fine." Sky chuckled. "Addison Porter, I know you too well for this."

"What?" Addi asked innocently. She unraveled her curly waist length hair. Today she was wearing it out.

"You are trying to distract me from asking you about Randy."

"True." Addi fluffed her hair and looked sideways in the mirror. She didn't look like a girl who had stayed up all night tossing and turning and thinking about Randy.

"You know, the one thing that I am thankful for reminding myself of is this hair thing."

Sky's sigh was heavy. "Okay, I got the point, you don't want to talk about Randy or this new mysterious guy you are dating. Please note that I will hound you in the next couple of weeks until you talk."

"Looking forward to it," Addi grinned, "but for now I am heading out to work. And please, for the love of all things good and right in the universe do not call your unborn child Simba."

"But I love the name." Sky chuckled. "I loved Lion King and Travis agrees with me that Simba Jefferson is a nice name."

"Good lord!" Addi groaned. "I don't know if you are serious or not but I don't think it is a good idea to be naming your kid after a cartoon character."

She hung up the phone and headed for the door. There was a slight drizzle, and she considered going back to get her umbrella.

"Nice day, huh?" Vanessa came out on the landing. As usual, she was in her gym gear and looked like she was heading out.

"Yes." Addi chuckled. "The question is, will it get worse? Should I get my umbrella?"

Vanessa looked out at the sky and then back at Addi. "It might rain, and you look so nice. You don't want to get wet and ruin your date with Errol this evening."

Addi looked at her with a frown. "You guys are pretty close?"

"He didn't tell you," Vanessa shook her head in disappointment, "he is sort of like my big brother. I went through a rough patch a couple of years ago, and Errol helped me out. I don't know what I would do without him. He literally saved me from doing something drastic..."

Vanessa bit her lip. "Errol is the best human being on the entire planet."

Addi nodded. "I hear you."

"And he deserves to be happy," Vanessa continued, "and since he is so interested in you. Please don't hurt my friend."

"We are not dating." Addi cleared her throat. "This is a bit premature."

Vanessa smiled. "There is a feeling I have about you, Addi. You are different. You will see past the superficial, and you will love him for his wonderful personality and his generous spirit."

Addi restrained herself from rolling her eyes. Vanessa sounded like she was advertising for Errol and didn't she know that Errol was into Selena?

"I am going for that umbrella," she said out loud. "Have a good day, Vanessa."

Vanessa smiled at her serenely, and Addi headed inside. Only coming out when Vanessa drove out of the parking lot.

****

Randy wasn't in office for most of the day. Addi was extremely happy for that. She didn't want to know if there was going to be any new tension in the air from last night. She just didn't want to face Randy right now, not when her emotions were in a state of flux. As it was, hearing him on the phone was enough torture.

He called at midday to ask her to fax something to him, and she did so. He called at two for her to arrange an interview with a guy he was thinking of poaching from another company as general manager, and then he called at five and told her that she could leave the office; he wasn't going to need her for the rest of the evening.

That was fine with her, her dinner plans with Errol were at five-thirty, and she had no idea where Jam Pub was. She had to call him twice to get directions. It was a little bit out of town and the traffic at that time of the evening was heavy. She turned the station to an evening radio program and was caught up in an interview with a much fawned over basketball star who was in Jamaica for a charity event. The announcer, Dawnette, sounded as if she was salivating.

Addi settled down to listen to the station, not because she was interested in basketball but because every other station was playing ads.

"It's Kenrick Douglas everybody," the radio announcer sounded excited, "they are calling him the next Michael Jordan in the NBA!

"Kenrick, tell us, why you are here in Jamaica and where can die hard basketball fans get to see you?"

Kenrick chuckled. "I am flattered that you think that I am the next MJ, Dawnette. I don't know if anybody knows this but my mother was born here and I vacation here all the time. I am not a stranger to this place. A couple of years ago I came out and stayed for two months right here in Montego Bay and got acquainted with the needs of some of the students at a particular school near where I stayed and I adopted them."

"That's so cool." Dawnette squealed.

Addi turned to another radio station at the same time; she had lost interest in Kenrick Douglas and his charity event.

The next station was playing Lauryn Hill and Bob Marley, Turn Your Lights Down Low. She turned up the volume and sang along.

****

She was late. Addi turned into the parking lot of the Jam Pub restaurant. It was a pretty little place. A giant Rastafarian statue was at the entrance of the building, and reggae music belted from the main building it had a big Jam Pub sign on it. It looked scanty in the half dusk.

There were three round buildings off the main building.

She could clearly see people who were seated and eating. The main building was obviously the bar section.

There was a big screen television in there, and a few persons were watching it. She headed for the main pub; a waitress greeted her at the entrance.

"I am meeting someone here?" Addi looked around but couldn't see Errol.

"Are you Addison Porter?" the waitress asked. "Errol is seated in the sea booth. Please follow me."

Addi looked around as she followed the waitress. She liked the atmosphere. She could distinctly smell the delicious scent of fried fish.

She was hungry by the time she reached the table where Errol was seated. She understood why it was called the sea booth, it overlooked the shoreline in the distance, and it was farthest from the main building with the throbbing reggae music.

It was quieter in the sea booth. There were five tables under this section of the restaurant. The tables were set apart from each other for privacy.

"The glorious Addison!" Errol greeted her in what she was beginning to think of as his penchant for high drama.

"The dramatic Errol Daniels," she replied quite unmoved by his flattery.

He was dressed in a white shirt, opened to the neck with a chain nestled around his neck. It glinted in the low light.

She could smell his cologne from across the table. It wasn't subtle, but it smelled good.

She had never really looked at Errol thoroughly, and tonight she studied him feature by feature, and then it dawned on her that he was quite good looking. He had more than a passing resemblance to Heavy D. Same complexion, round face, nose...

"You are making me squirm," Errol said smoothly, not looking one bit affected by her staring at him.

"I was just thinking that you have the look of Heavy D, the rapper." Addi leaned back in her chair; she was unexpectedly comfortable around Errol. He was easy to be around.

"I've heard that," Errol chuckled, "maybe because we are both heavy and have the same complexion?"

"Maybe." Addi smiled.

She waited until the waiter filled their glasses with water and took their orders before she spoke.

"So, here we are." She sipped some water and then looked at Errol assessingly. "I am not sure why I came."

"Because of the kindness of your heart." Errol chuckled. "You know that we are the only hope for those two to get it right. So we need to plan."

"I don't think we should interfere." Addi inhaled. "If Selena loved you, she wouldn't be going through with this marriage and Randy is not in love with me, not by a long shot."

Errol rubbed his fingers along the stem of his water glass before speaking. "I can't speak for Randy, but I do know Selena. She is a complicated and complex woman. She loved me once. She can do it again. She just needs to see..."

He sighed. "She is just a bit too..."

"Selfish, superficial, shallow?" Addi finished for him with a sneer. "I don't see why you love her if she is doing this to you."

Errol grimaced. "I do though; I love her. It is my curse."

"What about Vanessa?" Addi thought about how earnest Vanessa was with her compliments of Errol.

"What about her?" Errol frowned, looking uncomfortable.

"Aha," Addi grinned, she was on to something. "Vanessa seems to be your most ardent cheerleader."

Errol smiled. "She is, but our relationship is strictly platonic. Van was my personal trainer a couple of years ago when I thought that I had to get slim to...let's just say I had insecurities."

"About Selena and her shallowness?" Addi asked rubbing it in.

Errol didn't bother to answer, he just shrugged. "I could have lost the weight and gotten in shape. If Van hadn't gone off the deep end that summer I might not have gone back to my old self. I was making progress and dropping weight steadily. I was eating right, I even had some visible muscles and then..."

"What happened to Vanessa?" Addi was interested. She recalled Vanessa saying that Errol had saved her from doing something drastic.

"Kenrick Douglas happened." Errol leaned forward to her and lowered his voice. "You know of the basketball star?"

"Yes. I just heard an interview with him today!" Addi said excitedly. "He knew Vanessa?"

"He raped her," Errol growled. "Every time I see that freak on television I wish I could knock all his teeth down his throat and cut off his penis and stuff it down his...sorry."

Errol inhaled. "I know he is back in Jamaica for a charity event and acting like he is this magnanimous fellow who can do no wrong but I..." Errol curled his fist. "I hate what he did to Van."

"Calm down." Addi touched his hand briefly, "some things are grossly unfair, but you can't get too worked up over them. They will drive you crazy."

"I guess." Errol closed his eyes. "But I could have prevented this particular madness from happening. I canceled my appointment with Van that evening because Selena wanted someone to woo a tough customer at dinner. As usual, when

Selena said jump, I squeal how high."

Addi chuckled at his imagery.

"Unfortunately, Van had a friend who knew somebody who knew somebody who had connections and they were going to a Kenrick Douglas hosted party at the villa he was renting here in Mobay.

"It didn't take long for him to meet Van. He was in lust with her from the get-go. Van said he was high, and she tried to keep her distance, but he made his interest in her clear. A group of his friends forcibly carried her to his room, and the cretin raped her while they guarded the door and then they took their turn.

"When he was done, he had the audacity to suggest that she sleepover so that they can have some more fun. Van, of course, high tailed it out of there. She was a wreck after that."

Errol picked up his glass and sipped. "She, of course, didn't report it to the police. It was her word against a superstar baller. Her friends thought she was stupid for not spending the night, so you know they would be no help in the she said/he said game. She was quietly going out of her mind when I found her curled up and crying in a corner at the gym one evening.

"That was three years ago, we have been through a lot since. She went through a total shut down for a year. I lost my best trainer, nobody else was as effective as Van and trust me, she was not my first trainer. Van is just now getting back on her feet, but she is not the same. Either that or I lost the motivation from three years ago."

"Oh," Addi swallowed, "that's...I am so sorry to hear that about Vanessa. Now I understand why she speaks so highly of you."

"If there is a time in my life that I would redo, that would be it," Errol said wistfully, "I would have said no to Selena, stayed and done that session. Van wouldn't have gone to that party; I would probably be a smidge slimmer."

He patted his ample belly and then laughed. "Wishful thinking huh?"

"Not if you know a resetter," Addi said wistfully.

"A resetter?" Errol frowned. "What's a resetter?"

"Someone who can time travel in his or her lifetime. Resetters usually have a 't' in their palms." Addi waited for him to laugh, when he didn't she continued. "Of course the resetter has to find a pathway, usually a stone and then think of the specific date they want to go back to and then they are there with their memories of where they are coming from, but it will only last a while."

Errol didn't speak after she finished. The waiter came and took their orders, and Errol still regarded her contemplatively after he left.

Addi sighed. "Okay, forget it. I didn't know that telling you this would render you speechless."

"What do you mean by a 't'?" Errol finally asked.

"Huh?" interest in what she was saying was the last thing that Addi expected.

"The 't' in the palms," Errol said, "you mean two lines crisscrossing each other like a cross?"

"Something like that," Addi said. "Yes, exactly that."

"That's interesting, your theory. If only it were reality."

"Well, it is real." Addi shrugged. "I was a resetter myself."

Errol raised his eyebrow and was about to say something, but somebody at the entrance of the booth caught his attention.

"Oh joy, you wouldn't believe who just walked in."

Addi looked around and saw Randy and Selena. Randy had his hand resting on the small of her back, and they were looking quite loved up. Randy was in jeans and a white shirt that was opened at the neck. Selena's hair was out. She wore a lime green tailored summer dress, with matching shoes.

Addi turned around swiftly. They hadn't spotted them yet.

"We could go," she whispered to Errol. She didn't want to see Randy and Selena together, interacting like a couple in love. It could send her into the bowels of depression for days. It was one thing to hear about Randy and Selena. It was another thing to watch them interact.

"Are you crazy?" Errol looked at her a twinkle in his eyes. "Not on your life. This couldn't be more perfect if we planned it."

Chapter Ten

"**Y**our personal assistant is dating Errol?" Selena asked Randy sharply a few minutes after they were seated.

Randy frowned. "What?"

Selena was in the middle of relating her wonderful trip to Kingston. He wasn't sure he heard right.

"That girl, Addi. She is huddled over at the corner table looking pretty chummy with Errol. To your right. Don't look now." Selena hissed when he was about to turn around. "Is it okay for me to look now?" Randy asked after Selena fixated stare in the other couple's direction.

"Yes." Selena shook her head slightly.

Randy looked around. It was Addi; he would recognize her curly hair and her profile anywhere. Errol was saying something to her and staring in her face as if she were the last woman on earth.

He turned back to Selena and nodded. "That's her."

"But," Selena's voice was incredulous as if she couldn't

quite believe what she was seeing, "Errol doesn't date."

Randy curled and uncurled his fingers. He wasn't sure why seeing Addi so engrossed with Errol was causing him so much disquiet.

Surely she wasn't interested in Errol? But, why shouldn't she be? The guy had already sent her flowers, he was probably charming and made her feel beautiful and listened to her as she talked and did all of the things that were so important to women.

"He is a man, she is a beautiful woman," Randy said refocusing on Selena. "They are both single, why not?" He said this casually, but it caused him some discomfort.

"It's Errol," Selena looked at Randy with something akin to panic in her eyes. "Errol is...I don't know...always alone, perennially single, totally available."

"And now he is not." Randy forced himself not to look around again.

Selena was not exercising any such discipline. "They are holding hands across the table."

"Why is this so fascinating to you?" Randy asked irritably. He didn't want to think of Addi dating anybody; he wanted to pretend that this was not happening. "You were telling me about Kingston and your deal."

"I was, wasn't I?" Selena looked at Randy. "Do you think that they are sleeping together?"

Randy clenched his teeth and struggled not to swear. "Selena, come on let's not speculate about them, it's none of our business."

"Yes, you are right." Selena looked at Randy and smiled, but the smile didn't quite reach her eyes. "I can't believe he...okay, okay. The engagement party, how is that going? I hope you squared off everything with the planner."

"I was busy, so I asked Addi to do it." Randy sipped his

water that the waiter had poured without him realizing it, so taken up was he with the sight of Addi and Errol. Somehow it felt like the sparkle had gone out of the night. He felt uncomfortable and disturbed.

Selena asking about Addi and Errol sleeping together had opened up a line of thinking that was making him downright mad.

It had only been what, two and a half weeks?

Why would she be sleeping with Errol already?

For crying out loud, if she was thirsty for sex, he was available.

No, he wasn't. He squashed the thought as readily as it had popped up in his head.

"You asked Addi to make our party arrangements?" Selena asked incredulously.

"Yes. I didn't have any time for the inane details." Randy snapped, "I work too you know. When you run off to Kingston to pursue your deals I am not here twiddling my thumbs waiting for you to come back."

"It is our engagement party! I trusted you to give the planner personal details. I didn't expect you to offload it on your little secretary who looks like a shameless flirt. If I wanted my engagement party to be a circus event I could have easily asked the planners for that theme."

"Come on," Randy tried to calm her down, "Addi is not a shameless flirt, and she does have taste. She's a classy lady with an eye for things like decor and that kind of stuff. She is very competent at things like that."

"She looks like she is a competent gold digger," Selena hissed. "I am sure that she is only dating Errol because he is rich. I hope she knows that without me, he wouldn't be."

Randy looked at Selena closely. "My God, you are jealous of them."

"Oh shut up." Selena got up. "I am going to the ladies!"

Randy watched her retreating back and then looked at his watch. Ten minutes into their date and they were arguing about Errol, of all people, and things had been going so well.

She was happy when he picked her up at home. Now she was like a bear with a sore paw, or more like a jealous mama bear with a sore paw. She didn't want her precious doormat Errol to date anyone. She obviously liked his sycophantic sucking up to her and his slavish obedience.

If Errol had been with anyone else but Addi, Randy would personally go over there and congratulate him. His Selena fixation had been uncomfortable to watch, but he just wished that Errol hadn't chosen Addi to focus his attention on.

He glanced over at them again. They were talking animatedly about something. He wished that he could hear what it was. Then he realized that for the second night in a row he was sitting at the other end of a table watching Addi as she captured the attention of another male and with that realization came the knowledge that he so wanted to be the one who had her attention.

He shut down that rogue thought as he was doing with all the other uncomfortable ones that had been swimming around in his head.

****

Errol was almost giddy with success; his dinner date with Addi was more than successful, it had exceeded all expectations. If he were light on his feet, he would be skipping through the parking lot on the way to his car. Randy and Selena had looked miserable for the hour that he had covertly watched them in the restaurant. They had even left early, and Selena had not even had her dinner. She had picked around the delicious jerk chicken dish as if it were poisonous. Randy had twisted around to watch their table more times than Errol could count until he had been forced to wave to the poor guy.

If one dinner could upset the lovebirds so much, just a few days before the engagement party, he had a pleasant feeling that their wedding was not going to happen.

He walked Addi to her car and watched as she got in.

"It was fun." She grinned at him. "You are fun to be around, Errol."

"I do try." Errol winked at her. "Let's do this again. I don't know if you have an invite to the engagement party, but you could be my plus one."

"I am not sure." Addi pulled on her seat belt and avoided looking at Errol. "I wasn't planning to go even if I were invited."

"Come on," Errol cajoled, "you see how unsettled Selena was on seeing me with you and Randy, she was one part jealous and one part incredulous."

"I have to take your word for it. You never allowed me to turn around to look at them."

"Because it would have spoiled the misery they were having." Errol chuckled, "you just have to come to their party. We have a mere twelve weeks to break them up."

"You sure about this?" Addi asked skeptically.

"Absolutely." Errol nodded. "You and I make a pretty good demolition team."

"Okay then." Addi yawned and then covered her mouth quickly, "sorry, I am tired didn't get much sleep last night."

"Sleep well," Errol stepped away from the car. "Talk to you tomorrow."

Addi backed out of the parking lot, and he headed for his car. His cell phone rang, and he fished it out of his pocket. He hoped it was Selena so that he could wax poetic about Addi being a great date but instead it was Vanessa. She usually called him before going to bed. It had become a ritual of theirs.

"I sprained my right hand at work today," Vanessa said grumpily. "One of my clients fell on it."

"That sucks." Errol maneuvered himself into the car and panted a little. He was grossly out of shape even for a guy his size. He needed to get moving, as his doctor had been urging.

"You at the apartment?" Vanessa asked. "I want to open a can of soup. My left hand is not cooperating I almost cut myself trying to use it."

"No I am not at the apartment, I'll be there in thirty minutes. Can you wait that long?"

"I could ask your new girlfriend, Addi to help me, she seems nice." Vanessa chuckled, "I think I was overselling you a bit to her this morning."

"She is not a girlfriend," Errol laughed with her, "She is helping me to make Selena jealous. I just went on a date with her too, and Selena showed up at the restaurant with Randy."

Vanessa was silent.

"You still there?" Errol started the car.

"Yes," Vanessa mumbled. "I just wish you would forget about Selena in a romantic light. You are obsessed, and I hate that. I feel like a broken record. I have said this so many times before. I had high hopes for you and Addi. Why can't you give Addi a chance?"

"Because..." Errol drove out of Jam Pub's entrance. "I have to go I will be at your place soon, and then we'll talk."

He hung up the phone and turned on his CD player.

The first song on his blues CD was, At Last, Etta James. It was his anthem; one day he would play it with Selena in his arms.

****

Errol knocked on Vanessa's door a little after nine.

He looked out at the parking lot. Addi had reached home safely. He was parked beside her car.

His building was a five minutes walk from the Green Building; he should just leave his car down here and walk up the slight incline. He was too stoked to sleep and too conscious of how out of breath he was becoming.

Vanessa opened the door at the same time as he was thinking about exercise. She was in short shorts, and a stretched out t-shirt. Her right hand was taped together with a sling. She looked fit and toned with her creamy brown skin. She didn't need makeup. He admired her toned legs and then looked up into her pixie face.

"You want assistance ma'am?"

"This way." Vanessa led him to her kitchen and handed him the can opener. "You are panting."

She accused him while he opened the tin for her.

"I am a bit out of shape," Errol muttered.

"A bit?" Vanessa took the soup from him and then handed him a tin of tuna.

Errol made a face. "You are not putting the tuna in the soup are you?"

"No, that sounds interesting though." Vanessa grinned. "I am making a sandwich and then heating up the soup."

"I'll make your sandwich," Errol offered. He didn't mind doing it for her.

Vanessa sat down at the counter and looked at him as he busied himself around her kitchen.

"I have come to a decision," she said when Errol put the plate down in front of her.

"What?" Errol asked, grabbing a paper towel and wiping the sweat from his face.

"I am going to be your personal trainer again." Vanessa

pointed at him, "this is pro bono, and this is going to happen. I know you hate the gym, so we are going to have to do other things, like walking on the beach, swimming, whatever will get you moving. I will write you a meal plan, and you are not going to cheat."

Errol groaned.

"We made progress a couple of years ago, we can do it again," Vanessa said firmly, "I can't afford to lose you Errol. You are my rock, my best friend. If it weren't for that incident that messed me up, you'd be at a healthy weight again."

She shook her head and then glared at him, "I allowed you to have your own way for far too long. Expect me at your door five o'clock tomorrow morning."

Errol smiled at her earnest expression. "But your hand, remember?"

Vanessa held up her left hand and wriggled her fingers. "We'll just have to make do with these, and we are not going to be doing anything hand related."

Errol narrowed his eyes when he saw the two distinct lines in her palms. He forgot what Addi had called it again, recallers? Redoers?

He dismissed it as a fairytale and then focused on Vanessa. "Okay, no arguments from me. I'll be ready at five. Why is your apartment so hot?"

"My AC is acting up. It takes a while to get going," Vanessa muttered.

"Then I'll get you a new one," Errol said heading to the door, "no arguments. Consider this a barter."

"Fine." Vanessa got up and held the door open as he walked through. "Surely you can walk to your place. You don't have to drive."

"Yes, I was thinking of that," Errol grinned. "I'll get it in the morning. Goodnight."

"Goodnight." Vanessa watched as he lumbered up the hill and then closed the door.

Chapter Eleven

Randy was in a foul mood when Addi got into the office.

"Be afraid, be very afraid." Wanda, the receptionist, warned her before she even saw him. "He is acting like somebody stole all his money and he caught his girl in bed with the gardener."

Addi laughed. Wanda's imagery was funny. She still had a smile on her face until she reached her office and saw that Randy was sitting at her desk.

"We need to talk." He growled, as soon as she walked in.

"O...okay," Addi said nervously. Obviously, she had done something. She couldn't think what.

"Is it the Grange account? I did call him yesterday to arrange a meeting as you requested but he was not in. His secretary said that he was under the weather... had the flu."

"No," Randy frowned, "this is more of a personal matter."

"Yikes," Addi muttered. "What did I do?"

"You..." Randy inhaled. "You are Josh's little sister. He is my best friend. I feel that I have some responsibility toward you."

"I am listening." Addi folded her arms.

"You have been here now for what, two and a half weeks?" Randy looked at her balefully. "I don't know what kind of lifestyle you were living in New York, but I think I should warn you that Errol is not the right guy for you."

"What?" Addi was confused. Was he actually that worked up about the dinner date?

"I always thought that you would be more fastidious with your lovers." Randy looked like he swallowed something distasteful and hated every minute of it. "I am shocked that you are moving so quickly with Errol."

"Lovers?" Addi scowled at him. "What are you talking about?"

"You were at dinner with him last night, and when I came in I saw his car in front of your apartment, and this morning when I got up for my morning run, it was still there. I mean I am not judging you, and it is none of my business, but Errol is...how should I put this delicately, not into anybody but Selena."

"And you are okay with that?" Addi asked him astonished that he knew.

"What can I do about it?" Randy asked. "They are business partners. She depends on him to get stuff done."

"She uses him like her lap dog and abuses his adoration for her." Addi pointed out. "She is not a nice person."

Randy sighed. "They had their way of doing things before I got in the scene and it works for them. What I can't understand is why you would have a relationship with Errol knowing where his heart lies?"

"Maybe I am a glutton for punishment, and I like men who are otherwise involved with other women in some way or the other." Addi glared at Randy. "You are right; this is none of your business. Who I sleep with is none of your business."

Randy frowned. "It is my business. I don't like knowing that I hired a slut."

"A slut?" Addi widened her eyes and then picked up her handbag. "That's it! I am out of here. I quit!"

"What would you call it then?" Randy growled. "One night you were giggling with Linton Reid, stroking his ego, the next night you were doing the same with Errol Daniels and then sleeping with him."

"I did not sleep with him," Addi glared at Randy, "and you are jealous. Maybe you should examine yourself and see why that is. Ask yourself, why is it that I care so much about Addison Porter's personal life? It would be interesting to hear the answer."

She walked out of the office in a huff.

Randy walked her down and grabbed her hand. "You are not quitting. I need a personal assistant; you have to give me thirty days notice. You signed a contract, and you are sticking to it."

Addi inhaled and then exhaled, trying to calm herself down. Randy was looking truly livid because he thought that she slept with Errol. Mission accomplished. He was jealous. So what was he going to do about it now?

"You were out of order." Her voice lacked the kind of conviction it should have had because she was too busy thinking about all the possibilities of what Randy being this jealous meant.

"I am sorry," Randy said and then winced. "I saw Errol's car this morning, and I lost it. It's none of my business; your sex life has nothing to do with me."

"That's right." Addi hissed, "none of your business."

"I have examined myself." Randy leaned on the wall in

the passageway. He looked at her his gaze hooded. "When it comes to you, I lose some of my reasoning. I am so attracted to you it scares me."

Addi inhaled tremulously. *The admission. This was it.* She and Randy together forever.

"You should not have come back into my life, Addi," Randy said huskily. "We had our shot two years ago; you brushed away the idea of us being together so easily. I moved on. Now here you are. I can't imagine you with someone else without contemplating violence. It's contrary, it's maddening, it is... You are ruining my life."

"I am not!" Addi whispered. This was not quite the way she had expected the conversation to progress.

"Yes, you are," Randy growled. "I now understand why I had an affair with you for twenty odd years before you reset the timeline. You burrow under my skin, you lodge there, and you won't leave. I am going to fight this, Addi. If it is the last thing I do. Whatever I did before, however, I lived my life, it is not going to happen again."

He straightened up from the wall. "I have a couple of things for you to do for me today, they are pretty urgent."

And just like that, they were back to business, but for the little throbbing pain somewhere in the region of her heart.

****

"I can hardly walk," Errol murmured as they made their way slowly into the ballroom of the Palm Hotel. "I am pretty sure that Vanessa is out to kill me. So much for thinking that she was my friend."

Addi chuckled. "She is probably the best thing to ever happen to you."

She hooked her hand in Errol's and drew closer to him. He

was looking quite handsome. The tuxedo did an excellent job of hiding his girth, and his bow tie gave him a sophisticated air. When he arrived to pick her up earlier in the evening, she was surprised to see him.

Vanessa, of course, had been waiting with a camera ready and had taken their picture like they were off to the prom.

"I don't like Selena, but I am glad that she is getting married," Vanessa had confessed before waving them off. "Maybe now Errol can properly move on with his life."

Addi didn't share the same sentiments. She wasn't glad that Selena was getting married at least not to Randy.

Everybody deserved happiness, but Selena was not the one to make Randy happy. She was.

The thought had been ricocheting through her brain for the past two days. Randy was right; she had been the one to shut down the idea of them being together.

And now, she had to admit that was probably the worst decision of her life so far. The thought was killing her.

Her resetting efforts for her own life were based on a string of suppositions from the timeline before.

Fallacy number one: Randy was the reason that she was single and childless at forty. Fallacy number two: he had no problems cheating on his wife in the other timeline, so maybe he would cheat on her if she got married to him in this timeline. Fallacy number three: what she and Randy had could be easily replicated with some other man, some other place.

She had been wrong on all accounts. This time around she would probably end up single and childless at forty because she just had no good judgment when it came to relationships.

If she needed any evidence that Randy did not take his commitments lightly, she had it. For the past two days leading up to this engagement party. Randy was back to treating her like a contagious disease. He was professional and clipped with his responses to her. He made it clear that he was not going to let her ruin his life, even though he was attracted to her.

Randy was determined not to be a cheater.

And the final stupid fallacy that Randy could be easily replaced in her heart and head, well...that was clearly wishful thinking. He was unique. Her reactions to him were unique. She loved him.

The thought depressed her.

She took a glass of champagne from a passing waiter and looked around at the decor. It was tastefully done. Fresh flowers were everywhere, baby blue and silver colors were tastefully incorporated in the decor, and the live band was playing love ballads. A cabaret singer was at the front preparing to do a set. It was a nice atmosphere with a lot of glitter and pizzazz. She saw a few famous faces.

She was so busy taking in the atmosphere she didn't realize that Errol had come to a complete stop.

"There they are," Errol whispered, a forlorn quality to his voice, "the golden couple."

And there they were.

Randy in a tux should come with a warning. Lethal to females, prepare for swooning, fainting, and uncontrollable heart palpations.

Selena provided the perfect foil for him in her gold crystal dress. They looked good together. She clutched Errol's arm tighter.

"We shouldn't have come," she whispered to him.

He looked at her and nodded. "Want to go get drunk somewhere?"

"Alcohol is not on your meal plan." Addi smiled at him. "Nice try though."

"Selena is the reason why I am this fat," Errol muttered. "I put on a hundred pounds for every marriage she has."

"Ah, come on," Addi said. "Let us hang out in some quiet corner somewhere and bitch about how unfair life is to us. No need to resort to the munches."

"You are right," Errol muttered, and then he groaned. "There is Joe, Selena's very shady half-sibling. He conned me out of a couple of dollars, and he has been avoiding me ever since."

"Oh that's the guy from the investor meeting," Addi whispered. "He does resemble Selena."

"I forgot that he was at that meeting. He likes to think of himself as a businessman. How he makes his money does not invite close scrutiny. He is Selena's twin, and he is as crooked as they come," Errol snarled. "I have no idea how two persons can be so different. They are extremely close though. They are both overprotective of each other. It is sickening to watch sometimes. Selena will spend her last dime bailing out Joe from his mistakes. I don't think the idiot appreciates it."

Addi patted his arm. "The sibling bond can go deep. I think I would do the same for my brother."

"And that is why I am happy that I am an only child." Errol snorted, "no drama, no competition. And I have no cousins either. I am an only child of only children."

"Sounds lonely." Addi grinned.

"You mean heavenly." Errol snagged a glass from a passing waiter and lifted it to her. "I promised Vanessa I'd only take one glass. To us, may we be happy even if it is not with them."

"Here, here." Addi clinked her glass to his.

It wasn't long after that toast that Errol was soon dragged into a conversation with a friend from his university days.

Addi had no clue who they were talking about, nor was she interested. She drifted off to the side of the ballroom and inched closer and closer to the patio door. When the love songs started, and people started coupling up to dance, Addi was tired of standing conspicuously in the room like a lonely red beacon in her red dress while other people paired up and twirled around her.

She headed to the balcony and went into an unoccupied corner and looked over at the dark sea. It was probably an impressive view in the daytime, but at night it was just blackness.

She inhaled, and one by one removed the hairpins from her updo. She was ready to go home. She had no idea why she had tortured herself and come. The music filtered out to the patio.

A few people wandered out and then back in a ragged flow. She closed her eyes as the song Magnet and Steel came on. The cabaret singer was doing the version by Walter Egan as she had told the planner to incorporate.

With you I'm not shy, to show the way I feel, with you I might try, my secrets to reveal, for you are a magnet and I am steel.

Addi found herself rocking to the beat. She was so caught up in the song she didn't know she was under close observation.

"That's us," Randy said huskily, "magnet and steel."

Addi's eyes flew open. "Randy!"

"Am I wrong?" He came closer to her and skimmed a lazy forefinger lightly through her long curls.

"No." Addi shivered, a little tremor ran down her spinal cord he was so close.

Randy said ruefully, "I am at my own engagement party, and all I can think about is Addison Porter in the sexy red dress, looking both innocent and wicked at the same time."

"Where's Selena?" Addi whispered. "Won't she miss you?"

"No, not now." Randy chuckled. "She is trying to sell some ball player a luxurious property. This party is part celebration, part business. We are a pragmatic couple."

"Oh," Addi murmured thickly, "it sounds..."

"Unromantic." Randy shrugged. "I think I had one chance at being romantic and I missed it. I chose Selena as a partner because of who she is—practical, different. We know what to expect from each other. Romance is overrated."

"You love her?" Addi asked softly.

"Yes, I do." Randy nodded. "I love her shrewdness, her business acumen, her drive, her independence, her determination to succeed. That has to be enough."

"You sound like you are describing yourself." Addi pointed out. "Selena is female, Randy."

"Yes," Randy nodded, "Female, Randy."

"Maybe you both need something different. After all, marrying yourself is the highest form of narcissism."

Randy chuckled. "I love talking to you, Addi."

Addi smirked. "Likewise. Sometimes...when you are not calling me names."

"I said I was sorry, Magnet. Now that is a name that I think suits you." Randy moved even closer to her and stared at her in the half-light.

"You know you called me that before." Addi pushed her hair from her cheeks, "That was your nickname for me."

Randy touched her cheek. "Still the same old me, huh. I need to do something."

Her heart skipped a beat and then began to thud heavily. Her stomach clenched. The silence lingered.

The dim light accentuated Randy's chiseled features. His

dark skin was vibrant against the whiteness of his shirt.

Addi was so tense her muscles hurt. She couldn't make herself move, couldn't drag her eyes from him. She knew what Randy was going to do. She shouldn't allow it. They were at his engagement party.

Randy bent his head slowly. His breath fanned her cheek. He let his tongue dart between her parted lips, and she jerked and moaned and reached up for him.

He did it again, and her whole body leaped, electrified. Just one kiss, she promised herself, like a druggie craving her fix.

He pressed his mouth to her cheek, to her brow, to her lowered eyelids, teasing her with feather-light kisses until she strained up to him even more.

And then he kissed her lips. She melted to boiling point in seconds. He made love to her mouth with an intimacy that shook her.

And then he stopped.

People were moving in and out of the patio and laughing loudly.

Nobody was paying attention to them. Randy moved away from her.

"Just as I thought," he said huskily, "magnet and steel, you and I. Curiosity satisfied."

Addi slumped on the wall like a weightless sack of straw. All the energy was ripped out of her. "Did you just open Pandora's box?"

Randy raised his hands and ran it over her cheek. "It had to be done. Maybe this time the tension won't be so high between us. I have to go back and join my party."

"I am going home," Addi said hoarsely. "Maybe I should just pack and go to Mandeville and stay with my parents. This is one step closer to me being the other woman and you being an adulterer."

Randy paused. "No, that is not going to happen."

"Yes," Addi nodded, "it seems as if some things don't change. You even have the same nickname for me, that song was a test, I told the wedding planner to include it in the lineup. I wanted to see..."

Randy looked at her lips and then mentally shook himself. "I can change things before they get too far."

Addi nodded jerkily. "What are you saying?"

He stepped closer to her and kissed her hard on the lips. "Goodnight Addi."

And then he was gone while she stood there trembling, not daring to hope.

Chapter Twelve

Randy hit the gym at the apartment on Sunday morning. It was just eight o'clock, and the place was nearly deserted, except for an elderly gentleman who was running on the treadmill.

The radio was on and playing mellow reggae music. Randy headed for the weight area. He had a lot of pent-up energy even though he had not slept for more than two hours.

He had dropped home Selena at a little after three in the early hours and had come back home feeling empty, discontent, restless. He had been determined to go through his marriage with Selena and then he had kissed Addi at his engagement party. That kiss had made a mockery of his convictions, turned his world upside down. He wanted to be with Addi. There was no doubt in his mind.

He was smitten, and no amount of denial was going to get him over this.

Third World's version of Magnet and Steel came on as if in

response to his thoughts, and he smiled.

"Exactly!" He said it out loud and maybe a bit too vigorously. The man on the treadmill looked over at him curiously.

Randy turned to the weight rack and tried to look sane. He had known from the moment that Addi had re-entered his life that it was going to be like this. He had fought it, but he didn't want to fight anymore.

He wished he felt this way about Selena. It would have made life so much easier, but he didn't. Even before kissing Addi last night he knew it was going to come to this.

He would have to break the engagement. He had to do the right thing.

He was not going to marry one woman while loving another. According to Addi, he had done that before. He had no idea why he had allowed himself to do that before but this time would be different.

He was on his third set of bicep curls when Joe Burns sauntered into the gym. He was quite notably not in gym wear but his Sunday best. He did like to pretend that he was an upstanding churchman.

He headed straight for Randy and sat on the bench facing him.

"Hey, Randy."

"Joe." Randy greeted him coldly. He had always thought that there was something a bit creepy about Joe. He had shifty eyes, a less than genuine laugh. Joe always seemed as if he had some scheme going on.

If Joe weren't Selena's twin, he would not have thought that they were socialized in the same household.

"My sister loves you," Joe said conversationally, "and I love her, she said you make her happy. I like when she is happy."

"Is there a point to this rambling?" Randy wiped the sweat from his face.

"I saw you kissing Addison Porter at your engagement party last night." Joe flicked some imaginary lint from his jacket.

Randy froze. Not guiltily, no he was planning to come clean with Selena about that. He froze because Joe knew Addi's full name and he said it with such familiarity.

"From the moment she stepped on Jamaican soil we've been watching her," Joe said grimly. "That thieving pastor she almost married in New York has money for the family, and he knows where certain bodies are buried.

"We are waiting to see if she has any idea where the money is. The family believes she doesn't and that Garcia was just trying to throw us off the trail. What happened in her apartment in New York was just a warning. If she is hiding money for him, she'll be in trouble."

"What are you saying?" Randy could feel his heart hammering in his ears like a drum. Addi was in deeper trouble than he had thought. "You are with the mafia?"

"I admit to nothing." Joe fixed his dead stare on Randy. "And you will shut your mouth about this conversation or else..."

He let the threat sink in and then said in an almost conciliatory tone. "My sister is dear to me. I would never want her unhappy, so maybe you have nothing to worry about. You make her happy, so I encourage you to keep at it."

"What do you mean about Addi will be in trouble?" Randy asked urgently.

"Nobody messes with the family and live to tell the tale," Joe said simply, "family look out for each other. You get me? Take me for example. I love my sister. I help to keep her happiness level up in whatever way I can. I get her business deals. I even allow that pig, Errol Daniels to think he is winning big accounts because of his salesmanship only because he is a partner in their company."

Randy stared at Joe as if he had two heads. Any minute now, he'd wake up and realize this was a dream.

"I am not afraid of you, Joe," Randy growled. Dream or not, he couldn't stand by while Selena's shady brother threatened him.

"Not afraid of me?" Joe raised an eyebrow. "Maybe you should be. I am no longer small fry, Randy. I am now a very important point man in an international organization. When I say jump, people ask how high. I can get things done in the shadows that you know nothing about. It is not a good idea to cross me."

Randy sighed. "So you finally got a job in a criminal organization. Your parents would be proud."

"My parents benefit from my new job," Joe snorted. "I am the reason my sister's business is doing so well. I am the reason Selena could afford to buy them a new home. It's all because of me, and you know what, I kind of like being the behind the scenes person who waves a magic wand in everybody's lives to make things happen."

Randy stiffened when he heard that. All of Selena's business deals; her shrewdness and business acumen were manufactured by Joe?

The thought was sobering. Selena was dealing with a crime family. Did she know that Joe was her silent benefactor?

Was Selena in collusion with her twin?

"Don't hurt my sister." Joe got up unhurriedly as if he had just finished discussing the weather. "I am very much looking forward to the wedding. I already bought my tux."

And then he walked out of the gym, giving Randy a

satirical bow.

****

"Sorry I am late." Errol greeted Selena in the conference room on Monday. "I did not see your email about the meeting until late. Maybe you should have sent me a text."

"I will next time, still getting used to the text thing. It's fine that you are late though; the client is not here yet. Maybe he couldn't get up this morning. He loves to party." Selena was dressed in one of her pinstripe pants suits; she had a slash of red lipstick highlighting her lips. She was looking happy.

Errol wished that he could hate her or at least not feel so helpless around her.

"Hmmm." he sat down gingerly on one of the chairs. "This must be one important client for you to want me to sit in on the meeting."

"Yes, he is." Selena's eyes lit up. "I don't know if you saw him at the engagement party, I got a friend of mine to invite him."

"I didn't stay long at your engagement party," Errol grunted. "My date had a headache. I took her home. I was happy for it too; I think I might have pulled something while exercising."

Selena scowled. "Why do you even bother to exercise? You always quit anyway."

"Said the woman who wants me to have a heart attack and die so that she can have my half of the company."

"I wish you wouldn't say things like that," Selena muttered, "though I am quite pleased that you remember the clause in our partnership contract that says I get first dibs on your half of the business in case you die."

Errol frowned; he had forgotten that he had agreed to that

ridiculous clause. Their partnership contract had not been equitable. He had had no such right if Selena died first.

He had signed it like a blinded fool.

"Anyway," Selena said clipping her fingers, "I am just pointing out facts, you always start an exercise program or a diet program and then you quit."

"Maybe I have a reason to continue this time around," Errol said easily. "Maybe I want to be healthy for Addi."

"Addi is only with you for the money. She looks like one of those women who will flatter a guy and then milk him for all he's got and then leave."

"That's rubbish, that sounds more like you," Errol rejoined and then looked at his watch. "As much as I would want to stick around for your tardy client I have things to do."

"Wait," Selena said uncertainly, "are you really with that girl, Addi? I have never seen you date anyone."

"More fool me, maybe I was waiting for the right woman," Errol said lazily. He had never seen Selena looking so flustered. Maybe this making her jealous thing was working.

"I hope this new romance does not affect our working relationship," Selena said her voice clipped.

So much for her being jealous, Errol thought in despair. Selena wanted him to be at her beck and call without interruptions. He wondered if she had ever felt anything for him. Usually, after that thought, he would conclude that he didn't care, but this time he could not shake the impression that he was wasting his time.

This was a change. He had thought that Selena would forever ensnare him, but perhaps cracks were showing up in his obsession with Selena.

Why was he so obsessed anyway? The question came out of nowhere. She was a beautiful woman but so were a dozen other women he could think of in his life. She didn't have a particularly lovely personality nor was Selena kind to him.

He was like a loyal dog that was tied to the side of the house on a short leash, starved for food frequently, and whipped when his over-exuberance was inconvenient to his master.

He was uncomfortable with thoughts of himself as a starved whipped dog and Selena as his master, but the analogy was spot on.

It made him irritable, and the late client was not helping. "Who is this client?" He asked sharply.

Selena grinned. "You won't believe this, Kenrick Douglas, the basketball player. The Kenrick Douglas! He is looking for property, and we are his brokers."

"No!" Errol struggled out of his seat inelegantly.

"What?" Selena gasped. "It's Kenrick Douglas. The guy has a ton of money to spend, and he has friends. Lots and lots of loaded friends."

Errol slammed the desk in anger. "That cretin raped Vanessa. I told you this three years ago, didn't I?"

"You did?" Selena frowned. "I can't remember, it must have flown right over my head. Besides, what does it matter, it is business. When did you become a beacon of morality?"

Something in Errol froze.

He knew that for Selena business always came first, but this casual dismissal of such a serious crime was beyond the pale. A vein at the side of his head started throbbing.

"This company is not doing business with that man."

"Because of Vanessa?" Selena opened her eyes wide and stood up. Facing him across the table like they were gladiators on a battlefield.

She expected him to back down so she could have her way like she usually did, but that was not going to happen, this was Vanessa.

Vanessa had been more of a friend to him than Selena

had ever been. Sweet, loving Vanessa didn't deserve what happened to her. He did not care how much money Kenrick Douglas was bringing to the table.

He slapped the table hard.

Selena flinched.

For the first time in his working relationship with Selena, he was showing some backbone.

"We are not doing business with him!" Errol said it louder than he intended. He held Selena's gaze until she had to back down.

"You are going to call that rapist who should be behind bars, and you are going to tell him that your partner Errol Daniels is friends with Vanessa Rochester and he was the one who had to pay her psychiatrist fees and who had to stay up nights with her while she drowned in despair.

"You are going to tell him that if I see him face to face, I will take a bat to his knees and I will make sure that he cannot play basketball again."

Selena opened her mouth and then closed it. "Errol, I think that this overreaction..."

"Shut up!" Errol growled. He walked around to her side of the table. "Do what I just said and do not let that guy step on this property!"

Selena swallowed and looked at him fearfully. "No need to get so aggressive and over a girl who is not worth it. You are changing into somebody I don't recognize. I don't like this Errol."

"You haven't seen aggression yet!" Errol growled. "You will see aggression if I get locked up in a closed room with Kenrick Douglas. News flash! Today, I don't care that you don't recognize me. Maybe that's what you need, a partner to keep you on your toes. Not, 'yes man' Errol!"

Errol headed to the door. When he opened it, the staff

were scrambling to their places. They had probably started eavesdropping at the raised voices; something that was quite unusual in an office dominated by Selena.

"Good for you, Mr. Daniels," he heard someone mutter.

He didn't look to see who it was.

Chapter Thirteen

Selena called Kenrick Douglas as soon as Errol was out the door. She got his maid instead.

"Mr. Douglas just got out of bed," the helper said sourly, "but here he is."

She sounded like she was mad at him for something and then the phone was handed to Kenrick.

"Selena," he still sounded half asleep, "I am so sorry, can I come by at around one?"

"I'll come by instead," Selena offered. "Are you available at one?"

"Yes," Kenrick murmured. "Sure. I am free. Single and disengaged such a pity you aren't, you know. You are one hot lady, Selena."

Selena made a face at the phone. Kenrick Douglas was something else and definitely not her type.

"Have you seen my fiancé, Kenrick?"

Kenrick chuckled. "Yeah, I've seen him. I could take him

in a fight, but I don't want to be injured before the season starts. Great party, you guys, put on this weekend, though. See you soon."

She hung up the phone and headed for her office. *Yes, the guy was a flirt, but that didn't make him a villain.* She was not going to let Errol's little hang-ups prevent her from getting Kenrick's business.

Errol was allowing his overprotective nature to come between her and business. Vanessa Rochester was a nuisance. She had been a nuisance from the moment that Errol had met her. She wasn't going to let an incident that may or may not have happened interfere with her business deal.

She had no idea why Errol got so worked up over the scenario in any case. Vanessa had just been a personal trainer. Unless of course, he had felt something more for her at the time, which he probably had. He had started pulling away from the business and her around that time.

He had gained confidence with his little weight loss venture, and every other word involved Vanessa.

If you asked her, Kenrick Douglas had done her a favor in shutting down Vanessa for a while. At least that little period had served to refocus Errol on what was important—her and the business.

After that period the business had taken off, and they had expanded, and she had met Randy—he was the best thing that had ever happened to her.

Where in the world would she have found a man as compatible with her as Randy was?

He had no problems with the fact that this was her third attempt at the whole marriage thing. He was quite fine with her traveling at a moments notice for business. He listened to her go on and on about her business plans and accomplishments and was not bored of humoring her.

He was fine with the fact that the next couple of years she was all about her career—so no kids. She especially loved the fact that when she went anywhere with him, women literally stopped and stared. He was a fabulous lover too. Though they hadn't done any of that lately.

"Hold my calls, Yolanda, unless it's Randy." She glanced at her assistant on her way to the office.

"Sure thing," Yolanda smiled with her. "The party Saturday night was great."

"It was, wasn't it?" Selena nodded. "I had good planners. Thank you for recommending them."

"I loved the decor, all of those fresh flowers and the music and the food was to die for," Yolanda said enthusiastically.

Selena grunted and sat at her desk, feeling slightly resentful, the three things that Yolanda had pointed out were actually Addison's personal touches. She gritted her teeth in anger.

She was beginning to dislike that girl strongly.

She couldn't pinpoint why exactly. Maybe it was Errol's obvious adoration of her or the fact that Randy was so swift to defend her when she had seen her on that date with Errol or the fact that she had injected herself into her engagement party.

Selena frowned. Was it her imagination or was Randy feeling a little bit distant from her since Addison came on the scene?

No, she was imagining things. They had both been busy these past couple of weeks. She had so many things on her plate right now, and so did Randy. She was really looking forward to the honeymoon.

She had pushed Randy a few months ago to have them do a mini Caribbean tour. She hadn't heard from him if it was still on. But it would take some organization, and she was almost sure Randy had not done a thing about that yet.

Since Addison was such a great organizer, maybe she could arrange her honeymoon.

Selena picked up the phone. She needed to speak to Addison Porter, give her something constructive to do with her time.

****

"Hey Addi!" Vanessa greeted her outside her door when she was on her way to work.

"Hi!" Addi smiled, Vanessa was looking chirpy she was in sweatpants and a top which showed off her rock hard abs.

"Just getting in from my session with Errol." Vanessa wiped her brow. "I worked him out today."

Addi laughed. "He has been complaining."

"You should join us in the mornings. We walk on the beach road and then uphill." Vanessa said quickly, "not that I am implying that you are out of shape or anything because you look great!"

"But you are still trying to match make?" Addi looked at Vanessa knowingly.

"Am I that obvious?" Vanessa moved closer to Addi. "Since the engagement party, Errol is acting so depressed. This morning he was so low energy I had to go into his apartment and get him out of bed."

"He seemed fine at the party." Addi sighed. If anybody should be depressed, it should be her. She had a hot scorching kiss with the groom to be and had to pretend that it didn't happen.

Yesterday Randy was all business-like and efficient it had been sickening. She had foolishly thought that Randy would not go forward with this marriage. Somehow, she had thought that their kiss was going to be the beginning of something. He had insinuated as much.

Obviously, she didn't mean anything to him. She wasn't special enough to break his engagement.

Maybe she and Randy were not meant to be together in a legal binding committed relationship. She could not stick around if he were married. Goodness no, not the way she felt.

No wonder she hadn't slept last night. If she kept this up, she would be looking haggard in no time. Maybe she should walk with Vanessa and Errol. At least the exercise would make her sleepy.

"Do you know something?" Vanessa was looking at her concerned.

"Nope." Addi sighed. "I left the party early. Errol dropped me home."

Vanessa looked thoughtful. "Was it a good party? Did you see him and Selena interact?"

"It was okay." Addi shook her head. "I didn't see Errol and Selena speak at all."

"Mmmm." Vanessa sighed. "Maybe something else got him riled up. I heard that Kenrick Douglas was there, it was all over the Western Mirror today."

"Yes I saw him." Addi looked at Vanessa curiously. "He is the guy that..." She stopped. Maybe this was something that Vanessa did not want to talk about.

"The guy that raped me and then had his friends take turns, yes that's him." Vanessa puckered her brow. "I recovered, but I will forever be scarred by that beast demon. I still think he should rot in hell and I have dreams of slowly carving him up with a dull knife."

"Goodness, that's a lot of hate," Addi whispered. "Errol said you were recovering."

"I am recovering." Vanessa nodded, "I went through a very dark time. At least now I can function. I couldn't before. I tried to for a couple of months, and then Errol took me home to my parents."

"Did you report it?" Addi whispered.

"No, not initially." Vanessa bit her lip. "When they were done with me, they hosed me down like a soiled toy. They had obviously done that kind of thing before; they didn't leave any evidence behind for a rape kit. And then one of the sick morons dropped me at my building and gave me an envelope full of cash. I threw it back in his face. My friends thought it was so cool that I got to sleep with Kenrick Douglas, one of them told me I was lucky."

Addi gasped.

"Yeah, I am not friends with any of them now." Vanessa shrugged. "Errol is my only friend. And that's why I want to see him happy."

Vanessa shrugged. "Even if it is with Selena. But I'd prefer if it weren't Selena. She's too hard for him."

Hard. That was the word. And cold-blooded. The thought followed Addi all the way into the office.

Randy was aloof with her. Not that she expected anything different. He gave her a pile of resumes and told her to shortlist five for interviews with him.

He looked preoccupied.

"What's wrong?" Addi asked involuntarily.

He sat in the seat across from her desk and stared at her without answering. Addi could feel the tension in the air.

"You ever feel like wringing someone's neck, Addi?"

"No...Yes." Addi stammered. "I guess."

"I feel like wringing yours, that's all," Randy said it calmly, while he stared at her as if she had committed a crime.

The phone rang before Addi could ask what had she done.

"Randall Vassell's office." She answered automatically while looking at Randy.

"Hello Addison, it is Selena."

"Uh… Hello, Selena." Addi sat up straighter in the chair. She could not remember Selena ever calling Randy on the land phone, not since she started working for him.

"I don't know if Randy has mentioned it yet, but we are doing an island hopping kind of honeymoon."

"No, he didn't mention it." Addi looked at Randy who was now staring at her and the phone with alertness.

"Well from the first of June to the fifteenth should be blocked out on his calendar and since he is responsible for the honeymoon and I am almost sure that he has no time to plan it. Maybe you could do it."

"Me?" Addi squeaked.

"Why not?" Selena asked. "You gave your input in the engagement party. Write this down: Guadeloupe, St. Martin, Anguilla, Bart, Saba, and St. Vincent. I think we can squeeze in Mustique when we go to St. Vincent and the Grenadines. Be a doll and work out the logistics, hotel, airfare, ferry, tours, attractions et cetera. I am depending on you to work it out."

"But..." There was an ache in Addison's throat. She didn't know why Selena's breezy little list and her casual, 'work it out,' made her feel like she was near tears.

She lowered her gaze. Randy was looking at her intently now.

She cleared her throat, where was her backbone? She was not a martyr. "You work it out yourself. I don't work for you!"

She hung up the phone and jumped up out of the chair like she was scalded. Tears were in her eyes, and she didn't want Randy to see.

By the time she reached the door, Randy was blocking it. He closed it on her and leaned on it.

"What did she say to upset you?"

Addi looked at him tears swimming in her eyes. "She wants me to plan your honeymoon, you are..." her voice wobbled, "you are going island hopping."

The sob came out of nowhere. And then like an avalanche they kept coming.

She knew when Randy's arms encircled her; she snuggled into them and cried out her heartbreak like an infant.

She had no idea how long she stood like that. Locked to Randy, pressed close to him, the source of her hurt and the source of her healing.

"You okay now?" He asked when her tears abated.

She nodded. She felt like such an idiot.

He used his kerchief to wipe her face tenderly and then he put some distance between them.

"I'll plan the honeymoon." He bent his head and kissed her softly on the lips.

"No," Addi mumbled, "don't marry her, please. I am begging."

"I have to Addi." Randy stepped away from her regretfully. "I have to."

Chapter Fourteen

Day three of walking with Vanessa and Errol didn't do much in the way of helping her to sleep better, but Addi enjoyed their company.

It was obvious from the way that Vanessa and Errol interacted that they would make a perfect couple.

They couldn't see it yet, but she figured that if Errol was not so obsessed with Selena and Vanessa wasn't suffering from posttraumatic stress, they could have been an item. The ease with which they interacted with each together was admirable.

Errol often started the day by counting down to the wedding. It was becoming annoying. Addi found that she always gritted her teeth in irritation, maybe because she secretly started doing it too.

"Eighty-five days to go!" He announced when Addi and Vanessa walked up the slight incline to meet him at his apartment.

"I can't wait until they do it already," Vanessa said under her breath.

Addi declined to comment. The thought of the impending wedding was filling her with dread. She figured she would be at full capacity soon and that was when she would make herself leave the job. It was becoming even more torturous.

For the past week, Randy had been a model boss. He was getting quite adept at keeping his distance.

No personal conversations, nothing but business.

Even though sometimes in the last five days she found him staring at her in the most curious manner. She wondered what he was thinking. She had really let it go with that crying jag in her office.

"How is Queen Selena coming on with her wedding preparations?" Vanessa asked Errol, acid dripping from her tongue. Vanessa was obviously not a Selena fan. They should start a club.

"She has the wedding planner coming in every day this week, and they have lunch." Errol grimaced. "She bought the dress. It is a figure-hugging, backless number that will cause every male at the wedding a hard-on."

"Disgraceful," Vanessa smirked. "Don't you think so, Addi?"

"I think," Addi was careful not to bad mouth either Selena or Randy. Her private thoughts that their marriage was a mistake would stay private. "I think that whatever the bride wants to wear is up to her and her groom. She could even go nude it is her choice."

"Nude. Like the first couple, Adam and Eve." Errol nodded. "I can see that."

"But they were covered with God's light before sin entered the world." Vanessa rolled her eyes. "You two are too liberal for me."

"Although Randy and Selena can totally carry off a nude wedding," Errol said and then looked down at himself. "Obviously, I would not make a good nude wedding candidate, even though I lost five pounds in the last two weeks."

"When I am done with you, you can be a nude candidate at your own wedding," Vanessa said loyally.

Addi laughed at the two of them.

"I love weddings," Vanessa said as they made their way to the security gate at the apartment. "If it weren't for Kenrick Douglas, I would have been a virgin bride. I like the old way of doing things. I grew up in a strict Baptist family, and my dad fully expects my intended to ask him permission to marry me."

Errol looked at her regretfully. "I still blame myself for canceling on you that night."

"You have nothing to blame yourself for. The truth is, I blame myself for going to the party in the first place," Vanessa said contemplatively. "I was twenty-four and basically a house rat. I jumped at the chance to see a little bit of the party scene, to live a little, to shake off the last piece of the shy country bumpkin that I still had clinging to me. I was going to meet a big basketball star. It's funny now how excited I was."

"If I could re-live Thursday, August 8, 2000, I would."

Addi looked at Vanessa and smiled. "I told Errol this already, but some people actually can go back in time."

"Oh yes," Errol clipped his fingers, "I forgot to follow up on that time travel thing. Honestly, I thought you were pulling my leg. It sounded like a pretty fantastic story."

Vanessa stopped them, and they stretched. "Time travel, tell me about this, Addi."

"You probably won't believe me." Addi shook her

head. "Whenever I mention it people get skeptical. We are socialized to only accept what is in front of our faces. Anything outside of that is scary or mystical or strange."

"Try me," Vanessa grinned. "I grew up in a community in St. Thomas where strange things happened all the time. Take for instance, me. When I was very young, maybe four or so years old, I was running through a grassy common with two of my cousins, and I slipped and fell into a deep hole.

"Just like that, I disappeared. My older cousin is the one who is always telling the story; to be honest, I don't remember much. He said that they stopped at the hole and looked down. It was one of those bottomless holes that was supposed to lead to the sea. So he stayed behind, and my other cousin ran to get help.

"The cousin who stayed behind said he called and he called my name until he was hoarse. When my grandfather and a group of other people showed up, they sent down a rope into the hole; they even tied a flashlight around it.

"The rope seemed to go down for miles. They kept tying more rope to it, and it kept going down and down and down. By then everyone had joined the effort to find me again. My dad said he went back to the house for an extra rope he had in a shed when he saw me on the veranda, dry, unharmed, with not even a scratch. I told him that a man brought me home.

"I can't remember this of course, but to this day my disappearance and reappearance is a puzzle for the entire district."

"Cool," Addi grinned. "How do you explain that one, Errol?"

"I can't..." Errol shrugged, "but I will if given time."

"Oh and this one I swear is true." Vanessa was warming up to her storytelling. "I was thirteen at the time, St. Thomas was almost decimated in Hurricane Gilbert, my family are farmers, and we were hit hard. The family house is an old plantation house; it always needs repairs and one half of it, what we like to call the old half, was in no way ready for the storm that was Gilbert.

"In fact, we were prepared for it to go first. My father didn't bother to reinforce the roof or put any plyboard at the windows.

"During Gilbert, I got bored and restless. So I crossed the old dining room that we didn't bother to use anymore, everybody ate in the kitchen anyway. I went over to the old side, thinking that maybe I could get a glimpse of the storm. Daddy had battened up the other side tightly.

"My dad warned me not to go because I guess he envisioned the roof caving in from the winds or the whole thing collapsing but, while one side of the house was rocking and groaning like a woman in pain. The old side of the house had sunshine, and the landscape was different, it had more greenery. It looked more like a new house, the carpets were new, I smelled polish, there was a lot of old style furniture, and I saw a very old style looking newspaper on a side table, it read 'the Daily Gleaner, September 7, 1888.'"

Addi gasped.

Errol rolled his eyes. "Seriously?"

"As a judge," Vanessa crossed her heart in a juvenile gesture, "I read the headline myself, I still remember the ad at the top, 'Dr. Haydock's New Liver Pill for bilious disorders'. While I was there looking around and marveling at the many changes in the house that I thought I knew really well, a white lady in one of those dresses that you see in old time movies came behind me and started to scream.

"Gideon! Gideon! There is one of them in the house."

"I was so scared I ran across the house, and I was back in

storm conditions with my family. I told them that I went to 1888 across the dining room. They crossed, but they never saw what I saw.

"But my grandfather was the one to point out that the old half of the house was untouched by the storm. It's as if it had weathered the storm in a different time. In contrast, the newer side lost its roof. We had to stay in the older side for a few months after that."

"Fascinating." Addi looked at Vanessa with newly appreciative eyes. "Did you find out who Gideon was?"

"Yes. He was my grandfather's grandfather."

"For crying out loud," Errol protested.

"So I guess I met my great great grandmother." Vanessa laughed heartily. "I should have stayed and told her, hey in the future this is what your relatives will look like."

"You would shock the poor lady to death before her time." Addi chuckled. "So I guess telling you about resetters would not be an issue."

Vanessa shook her head.

"Resetters have a 't' in their palms. They can go back to any time they can think of once they make a connection with a pathway."

Vanessa nodded.

"A 't' like this?" She held up her left palm.

Addi stopped walking and then whispered, "Yes."

"That's where I saw it." Errol hit his forehead. "If I wasn't so preoccupied I would have mentioned it."

"But then there is this." Vanessa held up her other hand it looked like the average palm, with a few lines crisscrossing each other.

"Am I or am I not a resetter?"

"I don't know," Addi whispered. "This is a first."

"I am a half resetter," Vanessa said excitedly. "That's still something, right?"

"I guess. I have never heard of a half resetter," Addi said doubtfully. "I don't know if it is something or not."

"I want to know everything about resetters," Vanessa said excitedly, "everything!"

"And I will oblige," Addi grinned. "It is fascinating stuff. I was a resetter, I came back in '92, so I know this first hand."

"What year did you come from?" Vanessa asked excitedly.

"2017." Addi sighed.

"You two are crazy." Errol panted as he passed them. "I can't believe that Vanessa is taking this seriously."

"And I can't believe you didn't tell me that I am a potential time traveler." Vanessa stuck her tongue out at Errol.

"Half time traveler," Errol snorted. "If time traveling turns out to be a thing, please find me and let my younger self know that gaining weight is enjoyable but losing it is a hell of a lot of pain."

Chapter Fifteen

Seventy-one days to the wedding, Addi was secretly counting down just like Errol was. She had gotten in from work pretty late and had showered and was now sitting in the half dark living room. It was raining steadily, and she liked to watch as it hit the glass patio doors. To her, it was more entertaining than watching television.

She felt tired, not physically but mentally and emotionally. She needed a break from her constant whirling thoughts. This time of quietude was soothing.

She heard a knock on her door, a soft double knock. She groaned. She knew it was Vanessa.

It was two weeks since she had found out that Vanessa was a half resetter if there was such a thing. She had given Vanessa her unpublished manuscript which she had written documenting her resetting experience and the photocopied diaries of Gwendolyn Fisher Campbell.

With the new information, Vanessa was like an excited

puppy. Addi did not mind sharing the information with Vanessa it was fun to speculate about her palms and what it might mean.

Addi looked down at herself. She was in a simple top and really short boy shorts and her furry bunny house slippers. She was ready for bed. Vanessa wouldn't mind how she looked.

But it wasn't Vanessa at the door when she pulled it open. It was Randy.

He was dressed casually in jeans and a white t-shirt. His hands thrust into his pockets, his bulging biceps prominent under the short sleeve shirt. He looked at her tousled ponytail and her outfit and smiled.

"You look like fifteen."

You look fine. She wanted to say out loud. "Er...I was getting ready for bed." She said instead.

Randy nodded. "Your phone is off."

"Yes, sorry! I forgot to charge it." Addi raised an eyebrow. "You wanted me to do something?"

"No." Randy smiled, "your cousin is in labor. She said you should haul your butt to Kingston now."

"She's in labor! Goodness." Addi spun into the house and then turned back to Randy. "I have never driven to Kingston. I have no idea which road to take!"

Randy chuckled. "The last flight to Kingston is in forty minutes, Air Jamaica Express to the rescue. I already booked it for two. So, if you want to get going, Travis will send his driver to pick us up at the airport."

"You are coming with me?" Addi asked, her eyes wide.

"Yes, I have some business to take care of. Why not, kill two birds with one stone?"

"And there I thought that you were excited about the baby."

Randy gave her a half smile and then tapped his watch.

"Pack quickly. I am going to sit in my car, okay?"

He didn't have to tell her twice, Addi ran into the apartment and grabbed a travel bag. She got ready in record time.

When she joined Randy at the car, he looked surprised. "You sure you have everything?"

"Yup." Addi nodded.

"You still have on your bunny slippers." Randy grinned at her.

"Dang," Addi muttered. She went back into the house and got a pair of flats.

They reached the airport without a minute to spare.

It wasn't until they were seated in the plane that Addi relaxed. "It's kind of impossible to believe that there is no Air Jamaica in the future. Therefore no Air Jamaica Express."

She looked around and then her eyes connected with Randy.

"You remembered that?" Randy asked lazily.

"No. I wrote it down. I wanted to collect the calendars." Addi shrugged. "Must be something that I regretted not having in the future."

"Good idea," Randy relaxed in his seat and looked at her half drowsily. "I am curious about something."

"What?" Addi turned to him.

"How did Travis Jefferson and Sky get together?"

"You don't know? You were at the wedding."

"Yes, they emailed each other for years and then she finally met him when she went for an interview at his company etcetera... etcetera, but something he said, has me thinking. He said, he has known Sky and loved her for most of his life. Isn't he older and where would he have met her? I mean they do not travel in the same circles."

"He is a resetter," Addi answered. "Before he changed his timeline he was in a wheelchair; Sky was his student at

Mount Faith University. They fell in love then."

Randy frowned. "There are more people like you out there?"

"Yes," Addi grinned, "apparently."

"So how far back did he go?"

"When he was ten, I think. Sky wasn't even born yet."

"And he waited for her?" Randy asked incredulously.

"Yes," Addi sighed, "he waited for her...it's so romantic."

Randy nodded. "It actually is. They had to fall in love twice and under different circumstances. Talk about love standing the test of time."

"Yes," Addi turned away from him. She had gotten the same chance with Randy and had opted for something else. She could practically hear his mind ticking over as he thought about that.

"I wish I hadn't given up so easily when you turned me down two years ago." Randy sighed. "I wish we had taken our second chance. Obviously, you and I also have the kind of pull that can stand the test of time. We are drawn to each other. I can't shake my feelings for you, Addi."

Addi turned back to him and swallowed. "We still have time. You can still get out of the marriage."

"No, we don't have time." Randy cupped the back of her neck and looked at her with such a blazing longing it had her gasping. "I can't just leave Selena, not now. Not without some severe consequences to someone close to me."

"What kind of consequences?" Addi whispered. "What are you talking about?"

He brought his face closer to her until they were nose to nose. "Let's just say I have to keep my commitment to Selena. It's too late to back out now..."

"Randy..." Addi splayed her hand on his chest; she could feel the thudding of his heart under her fingers, "talk to me."

Randy covered her hand with his and closed his eyes. "Tell me about Devin Garcia, your ex-fiancé."

"Why?" Addi pulled away her hand, "That's all behind me now."

Randy cracked one eye opened and looked at her. "Humor me."

"There is nothing to tell." Addi shrugged. "We met in Paris. I was a model; he was visiting with his family."

"When did you find out that he was a criminal?" Randy rasped. "Do you have money hiding for this guy?"

Addi glared at Randy and then looked around. There was nobody seated within hearing range.

"No, I didn't know that he was a criminal. He was an upstanding Christian guy, one of the good ones. That's what I thought! And no, I am not hiding money for him. Why would I do that? That would make me an accessory to his crimes."

Randy had his eyes fixed on her now as if he was trying to ferret the truth out of her. She wanted to yell at him that she was telling the truth and she found it quite offensive that he didn't believe her.

He was silent after her statement, and then he closed his eyes. The silence between them stretched uncomfortably.

"Did you sleep with him?" Randy asked after a full five minutes.

"No!" Addi squealed. "What kind of girl do you think I am? You assume I sleep with everybody."

Randy chuckled at that. He opened his eyes and stared at her for a long time as if he were cataloging her features. "I am jealous of every guy you have ever been with."

"That means you are jealous of nobody." Addi twisted to her side and turned away from him, "I am still waiting for the right guy."

Randy made a choked sound.

Addi looked at him. "What?"

"I am the right guy," Randy touched her cheek, "and you are the right girl, but we are in a right mess."

"I don't understand," Addi pleaded with him. "Why are we in a mess and why can't you just leave Selena?"

****

"Why can't he just leave Selena?" Sky and Addi were finally alone in the room. Addi sat in the chair beside Sky's bed. The Jefferson clan and the Porter clan had all done their familial duties and come to greet the newest family member.

Travis had taken the baby to the great room with his father and brother, and the three of them were acting like they had never seen a baby before.

The Selena question was at the forefront of her mind like a song on repeat, and she asked it out loud to Sky now. She couldn't take it back even though it was unfair to Sky.

Sky was tired and drowsy. Though she had made the whole birth process thing look easy.

Travis had brought in what looked like an entire hospital of nurses and doctors to attend to her. She had a relatively easy and quick birth. Addi had almost missed it. By the time she had reached the house the night before, it was over. Simeon Miguel Jefferson was in the world. He had a head full of hair, and he was red and wrinkled, but he was the most beautiful baby she had ever seen. Not that she paid attention to newborn babies.

Sky and Travis were over the moon happy.

And here she was like a wet blanket fussing over something that she had allowed to happen. She wasn't surprised if Sky pointed that out to her.

But instead, her cousin looked at her drowsily and grinned.

"You finally came to your senses about Randy. That's good, finally."

"Not good." Addi pouted. "It's bad. Didn't you hear what I said? He won't tell me why he won't end it with Selena. He says he has to protect someone close to him."

Sky narrowed her eyes at Addi. "Really? Who marries a woman to protect someone else? That's ridiculous!"

"Right. That's what I thought," Addi mumbled.

"He will come to his senses," Sky predicted. "Randy loves you. When you turned him down at the wedding, he looked shattered."

Addi covered her face with her hands. "Can you please not remind me of how utterly stupid I was that day?"

Sky chuckled. "Okay. Where is Randy now? He told me he was flying over with you when I called last night."

"He is at the Pegasus. That's where he stayed last night. He said he has a meeting with a friend of his from the company he worked at before."

"Hmmm. Well, I hope he knows he has to come and see Simba before he goes back to Montego Bay."

****

Randy had breakfast in the hotel dining room and waited patiently for his friend Brian to join him. Brian was a retired FBI agent who still had his fingers on the pulse of the security. He had to find out what was going on with Joe.

He was feeling edgy. He hated feeling this way. The woman that he loved had ties to a Mexican drug cartel, and the woman that he was about to marry had ties to the same cartel.

"What have you gotten yourself into buddy?" Brian sat

before him. He placed a file jacket on the table and gave Randy a mock scowl.

Randy hadn't seen him enter the room. He had been so engrossed in his thoughts.

"I don't have a clue. How is it going?" Randy asked for more tea and gave Brian the once over. "You look like you've been spending many hours at the beach and drinking too much beer."

Brian was nut brown, his casual shirt was opened to reveal a sunburn mark on his chest, his blue eyes sparkled from his deeply tanned face, and his gut looked wider than Randy remembered it.

He looked like a typical tourist without a care in the world, but looks could be deceiving in his case. He used to be one of the best intelligence officers in his field.

"You are right. I spent a solid three weeks on the beach in Portland with Julie. We lived in a hut, drank coconut water from the shell, caught our own fish, and bathed in the rain. I felt like a regular Robinson Crusoe, except for when I went down to Marty's Bar and hung out with the fishermen. I drank more than my share of Heineken. If you had called me before last night, you wouldn't have gotten me."

"I did call." Randy waited for the waitress to serve the tea.

"Sorry about that, man." Brian took a sip of his tea and grimaced. "What the hell is this?"

"Cerassie." Randy chuckled. "Julie never fixed that for you in the bushes?"

"No," Brian made a face. "Even if she did it would have been loaded with two pounds of sugar. My girl is heavy-handed with sugar, salt, oil, and sex. I tell you, if I reach my sixty-first year standing, it will be a miracle."

Randy chuckled. "You two still strong?"

"Yes of course, why not?" Brian grinned.

It was a rhetorical question. Julie and Brian were opposites in every conceivable way—race, age, temperament, and looks. It was a miracle that they were still together.

"So tell me," Randy said, "what have I gotten myself into?"

"Deep fecal matter." Brian pushed the tea aside and took a file from his knapsack. "We are talking Mexican drug cartel, the Ramirez family. Ever heard of them?"

"No, how could I?" Randy frowned, "I feel like I am in the twilight zone."

"The Ramirez family is one of the most powerful crime family right now." Brian tapped the file jacket. "That name sends shivers up many a criminal spine. The family has their fingers everywhere, drugs, are their mainstay."

"Are you serious?" Randy took a sip of orange juice and then squinted at Brian, "if this is a joke it's not very funny."

Brian sighed. "My contact at the Bureau is not a man known to dabble in comedy. This is what I got at short notice. This is the unclassified stuff."

Brian pushed the file over to him.

"The Ramirez family have a legal business network, and they have a drug network. They are smart. They don't flaunt their cash. They rinse their money in places like mega churches. Like that church in New York that Devin Garcia was heading."

Randy opened the file, and there was a black and white headshot of Devin Garcia, the man who Addi had unknowingly gotten herself involved with.

He was good looking, Randy supposed. His face did not shout thug on the down low.

"Garcia got greedy," Brian said, "and he foolishly tried to rip off the family and then he got caught by the Feds for fraud. So that was a double blunder.

"The FBI has him in some undisclosed location. The family

is short over 70 million dollars of their money. I speculate that Garcia told someone that Addison Porter is the only means of getting back that money.

"That is why they left her alive, and that is why she is still being monitored, just in case...they may have investigated her thoroughly and found that Garcia is lying but they are still keeping an eye on her."

Randy swallowed.

"That brings us to Joe Burns. He joined their criminal network three years ago. I suspect he was chosen because he has several criminal connections on the ground here in Jamaica. Your brother-in-law to be has the nickname of Cat Man. Very stealthy. The FBI and local law enforcement have an eye on him."

Randy groaned.

"I know it sounds pretty grim." Brian scratched his jaw. "They are expanding in the Caribbean and property is their latest thing. Selena Burns and her partner Errol Daniels have been acquiring property for them. They want to extend their Caribbean reach and build luxurious hotels here."

"My goodness." Randy breathed. "So all those huge deals that Selena and Errol have been doing lately..."

"Courtesy of the Ramirez family and their network of businesses." Brian nodded, "but that's the legal side of their operation."

Randy laughed mirthlessly. "I can't believe this. Joe was boasting that he was the one who was making his sister successful. He was right."

"Yep," Brian raised a brow. "The question is, does she know?"

"I doubt it." Randy shook his head. "Selena is pure ambition. She doesn't have a criminal mind. She works hard; she loves the cut/thrust world of business."

"Her brother is a problem especially because he is in bed with the Ramirez family." Brian gingerly picked up his teacup and then put it back down. "I wouldn't marry her if I were you. Unless she is willing to cut all ties with him."

"The irony about this whole situation is that I changed my mind about marrying her. I realized on the engagement party night that I was making a huge mistake." Randy sighed.

"Well I realized before that, from the first moment I saw Addi again but I had convinced myself that I loved Selena because the two of us were so compatible. And I preferred the comfortable routine that we had settled into versus the tumultuous agony that Addi encourages by just being in the same room with me. I kept hoping for it to die."

"That kind of feeling never dies." Brian reminisced. "I have lived six decades on this planet, and I have only ever encountered that with Rebecca. Of course, she is happily married now and all... she's a grandmother too, but let me tell you, right here," he pointed to his heart. "There is a tender spot."

Randy winced. In a couple of years, he would probably be Brian, pumped full of regrets.

"Joe actually told me that if I don't marry his sister, he would kill Addi." Randy tapped the table impatiently. "I don't know what to do now."

"I'd take him seriously." Brian shrugged. "You can call his bluff, but Cat Man is dangerous and pretty smart. I wouldn't risk Addi's life that way. His crimes are arranged to look like accidents. He is running circles around the local cops in Montego Bay."

"I can't just leave Addi alone in the middle of this," Randy murmured. "She is so vulnerable right now."

Brian scratched his chin. "If you want to play this by the book, you can hope that Devin Garcia tells the Ramirez family where their money is and then she'll be of no interest to them.

"As for Joe Burns threatening to kill Addi if you don't marry his sister, I don't know...tell Selena about the threat. End it with her. If she is not a criminal as you say, she will tell her brother to butt out of her business, but if she is, you would have gambled with Addi's life."

"I don't envy you, man." Brian sighed. "You should have found a woman like Julie who is uncomplicated and whose one joy in life is living for her man—no drama, no intrigue, just a steady supply of sugar and sex."

Chapter Sixteen

Randy was silent on the way back from Kingston. They arrived in Montego Bay on an evening flight after spending the day with Sky and her family. It had been an effort to pretend to be happy. Addi was laboring under the same malady as well; she had appeared withdrawn and low key, which was totally unlike her.

She did not attempt to engage him in conversation, and he was happy for that. He didn't know if he should tell her about the threat on her life. It would only freak her out and make her conscious of all the sounds that went bump in the night.

He was going to have to order a discrete security detail for her. It might not be necessary once he married Selena, but it would make him feel better.

He turned on the radio when they got into the car, filling the space with music.

When he reached the apartment, Addi turned to him and

then cleared her throat.

"Randy, I decided..." her voice was husky and low.

He tensed up waiting for the rest of what he was anticipating to be bad news.

"I can't keep on working for you." She turned to him, and he was arrested afresh of how much he would miss her.

Addi had grown on him, needled her way under his skin and nestled there. He had gotten it right in 2000 when he had declared that they should always be together because the thought of him not seeing her every day. The thought of her living her life with someone else was panic-inducing.

"I was expecting this," he said out loud. He didn't want her to see his devastation at her decision.

Addi nodded. "It would be crazy to stay."

"Yes, it would be." He drummed the steering wheel impatiently. "It would be an emotional roller coaster for both of us. One day, something would snap, and we would be locked in a passionate kiss and then who knows..."

"Consider this the beginning of my thirty-day notice." Addi looked at him so sorrowfully he felt like confessing all to her and then what...suggest that she be his mistress?

She deserved better. Selena deserved better.

"Find a replacement, and I won't hold you to the thirty days." Randy's voice was husky. He stared at her lips almost transfixed and then dragged his eyes from them.

It didn't help that R. Kelly' song, *If I Could Turn Back The Hands Of Time*, started playing on the radio.

"How appropriate," Randy murmured. "Resetter music."

Addi cracked a smile. "What would you do if you could turn back the hands of time?"

"When I saw you in 1999 in New York, put my ego aside, laugh at your paltry attempts to keep me at arm's length. I'd drag you to the nearest church and get married to you before you could even think or speak, or 2000, at Sky's wedding, I hadn't met Selena yet, you were just three months in with that Garcia guy...I wouldn't be a gentleman about you keeping me at arm's length either. I wouldn't have watched you walk away. I would have said, Addison Porter, you are being ridiculous, there are no guarantees for the future, for God's sake don't walk away."

Addi turned to him. "Hopefully I'd listen."

"Hopefully," Randy sighed, "but you are so stubborn who knows, maybe we would end up right here anyway."

"And that's the issue with do-overs, redoing the past is fraught with its share of pitfalls."

Randy touched her cheek. "Maybe, if we always chose each other no matter what, no matter when we wouldn't find ourselves in this pickle."

Addi picked up her bag. "Now he tells me. See you tomorrow. I'll start looking into my replacement along with the new general manager."

Randy nodded. "Sleep well, Addi."

"I doubt that." She left the vehicle and headed to her front door.

She dropped her key several times. Randy didn't dare to get out of the car to help her. He knew where this would all end. He knew his limitations.

When she was finally inside, he closed his eyes. He would take a minute before he went upstairs.

****

"It doesn't look like he is cheating on me." Selena looked at her brother uncertainly.

They were sitting at the far end of the parking lot when Randy parked his car. They watched as he and Addi conversed briefly and then she went to her apartment.

There was nothing inappropriate going on there. At least not now.

"But you said she refused to plan your honeymoon and hung up on you." Joe glanced at Selena. "They went to Kingston together, and I did see them kissing at your engagement party."

Selena sighed heavily. "I wish you hadn't told me that."

"I could get rid of her for you," Joe said it without expression. "The family just has me keeping an eye on her just as a precaution. She is not that important to them."

"But how would Randy react?" Selena asked. "You foolishly went and threatened the girl and told him that you were watching her. How stupid could you be? If you got rid of her as you say, he will suspect you."

Joe grunted. "How can you threaten someone if you don't tell them how dangerous you are? Randy was going to dismiss me without a second thought. He would have left you. I heard him call her Magnet. You know the song magnet and steel?"

"For crying out loud, of course, I do!" Selena groaned. "I was talking to Kendrick Douglas at the time about some property. I remember him remarking that he loves the song."

"You were so busy chasing that baller's business that you ignored your man," Joe sniped. "I don't understand you, I set up all of these accounts for you, you don't need to be thirsty. That baller guy is small fry."

"You really are delusional." Selena turned to her brother, "I got those accounts because I am friends with Nico Ramirez. We were good friends at college when I went for my Masters. You are the brawn in this little arrangement, Joe. I am the brains."

Joe grinned. "I do chauffeur the investors around. Hence, I am the point man."

Selena snorted. "Whatever story makes you feel better. Listen, don't mess with Addison Porter. You are out of your mind if you think I am going to endorse murder or whatever it is you meant by getting rid of her. I wish you weren't such a psychopath."

"And if Randy leaves you for her?" Joe asked slyly, "what then?"

"Then nothing," Selena said irritably. "Let's stop talking about this."

"Weren't you the woman who was bawling on my shoulder earlier when I told you about them kissing?"

"I don't want Randy to marry me because he feels obligated or threatened." Selena inhaled. "I want real love, the true kind. I am thirty-two and down two husbands, Randy is the real deal."

"Too late," Joe snorted. "You may have had that but that girl is his magnet, and I did threaten him. He'd marry a pig to keep her safe."

"I hate that song now," Selena growled.

"I like it. The reggae version reminds me of cold beer, the beach and lots of hot girls." Joe leaned back in his car seat.

"You have simple tastes J, I wish I were so easy to please, but I am not." Selena pushed back her seat and put her foot up on the dashboard. "All I want is to be happy. Lately, all my plans are going wonky. First, Errol now Randy."

"Errol," Joe snorted, "I told you to pull out of your partnership with him a long time ago. You don't need him."

"I did before the Ramirez family decided to expand in the Caribbean. He was the one getting the huge accounts; he was getting too big for his britches implying that he was going to leave. I slept with him for a month to keep him in line. Now the idiot believes I had some grand love for him."

"But now he is a nuisance," Joe sneered, "I could arrange

for an accident..."

"No, what's wrong with you?" Selena elbowed Joe. "Errol is still useful. I'll let you know if that changes. I should go up and say hi to Randy."

"I am not waiting for you while you play with your lover. I have things to do. I'll drop you home, so you get your car and come back."

"There has been no playing with Randy since Addison came on the scene." Selena looked at Joe fretfully. "I wonder if he still loves me?"

"Don't know." Joe shrugged. "I am not acquainted with the finer feelings."

"I couldn't take him not loving me," Selena said coldly. "I am not sure that I could live with seeing him happy with someone else, flaunting it in my face. If it comes to that, I am sorry, but one of us has to leave town."

"Hell hath no fury like a woman scorned. I'll off him with pleasure." Joe grinned. "I'd poison him like I did Cassius Green...make it look like an accident."

"Do you have to bring that up?" Selena sighed. "I feel guilty when you do. I shouldn't have suggested that hit."

"You should feel guilty," Joe cackled. "You told me to get rid of Cassius so that your precious Randy could own an insurance company."

"I didn't mean for you to kill him and I didn't mean kill Randy either. Oh shut up and take me home. I'll see Randy tomorrow," Selena said sourly.

****

Vanessa exhaled big gulps of air as the car drove off. They had no idea that she was standing there. She had heard it all. Her hands were shaking. Her head was thrumming. She looked across at the well-lit apartment block and willed her feet to move one after the other, but she couldn't move.

She had carried her garbage to the garbage house and was on her way back when she had seen Selena in the passenger seat of a car with a guy who she now knew was her brother. She was going to sneak past the car, but something about the furtive way they were behaving had her inching closer to the vehicle. She was thankful that she was wearing black leotards and a black hoodie.

And now she was trembling with the after reaction of someone who had just encountered something malignant.

Selena was just as evil as she had always sensed that she was. The thought gave her little comfort.

Vanessa hurried towards her apartment and locked the door. What was she going to do with this information?

Tell Randy? Tell Errol? Tell Addi?

She was not going to the authorities with this. She remembered the hard time they gave her when she reported her rape.

She sat in her living room and hugged her legs. What on earth was she going to do?

Chapter Seventeen

Vanessa called Addi earlier than her regular waking up time. Addi looked at the clock and then double-checked. It was just four o'clock, and it was dark outside. She answered the phone groggily.

"You okay, Van?"

"We need to talk." Vanessa sounded solemn. "Come over to my apartment."

"Now?" Addi asked incredulously. "You mean this could not wait until daylight?"

"I'll give you ten minutes," Vanessa said her voice sounded tense. Addi didn't bother to argue; whatever it was must be pretty serious.

She pulled on a green tracksuit and washed her face.

She didn't need to knock on Vanessa's door. Vanessa was waiting for her it seemed. She pulled it open as soon as Addi stood in front of it, and then she locked it behind Addi.

She looked disheveled. Her hair was in disarray around

her head as if she had pulled her fingers through it too many times and her nightshirt which reached her knees was buttoned unevenly.

"Okay, here I am," Addi said looking around the space. It was her first time in Vanessa's apartment. There were pictures of birds everywhere and bird patterns on her curtains.

She sat on the sofa gingerly while Vanessa paced before her.

"I couldn't sleep," Vanessa shook her head, "and I couldn't get Errol on his phone. And I started to fret, you know, what if something happened to him?"

"You tried his landline?"

"Of course." Vanessa looked at Addi with exasperation. "I am not paranoid for no reason you know. Addi...I am...I don't know how to say this; I overheard the most bizarre conversation when I went to take out my garbage."

"Okay," Addi encouraged her.

"You kissed Randy at his engagement party didn't you?"

Addi stiffened. "Yes."

"And he called you his Magnet?"

Addi nodded and then groaned. "Who saw us?"

"Selena's brother, Joe," Vanessa whispered that information almost fearfully, "Addi he is a hit man."

"Hitman?" Addi widened her eyes.

"As in criminal." Vanessa sat on the carpet and then hugged her legs. "Addi you are not safe, Errol is not safe. Randy is not safe."

"What do you mean?" Addi's head started to throb instantly.

"Cassius Green. What do you know about him?"

"Nothing, except for the obvious, he owned the insurance company and died without a will." Addi whispered.

"He died of poison, last year August. Joe poisoned him so that Selena could convince Randy to buy his company.

Apparently, she suggested that it would be nice to get rid of Cassius Green, and poof, her magician-hit-man-brother made it happen." Vanessa inhaled raggedly.

Addi gasped. "No."

"Yes." Vanessa nodded. "Oh yes. What do you know about the Ramirez family?"

"Wait a second." Addi's head was still reeling from the Cassius Green revelation. "They are...they are the people that my ex-fiancé stole money from."

"Joe works for them." Vanessa ran her fingers through her hair, and then swallowed, "Addi they are still watching you."

"What?" Addi asked hoarsely.

"Joe offered to kill you for Selena because you are competing for Randy. He threatened Randy that if he left his sister for you, you would die."

Addi stared at Vanessa in dreadful silence. She couldn't process this. Not this. This was a dream. It had to be.

"Errol is not safe either, three years ago, he was the one pulling in the big accounts and now that Selena is working with the Ramirez family, he is no longer as useful to her. Initially, when that happened, she slept with him so that he wouldn't know what was going on. His head was so high on cloud nine thinking that Selena was the love of his life that he didn't realize that most of his clients were questionable.

"As for Randy, he had better continue to love Selena because she has a habit of telling murder-happy-Joe everything. And he loves to fix things for his sister."

"Good Lord." Addi breathed.

"I couldn't sleep, I had to tell somebody." Vanessa finished speaking apologetically.

"So that was what Randy meant when he said that he couldn't end his relationship with Selena because he is protecting someone close to him?" Addi whispered the statement in a half daze and then rubbed her eyes. Vanessa was still looking like a crazy caricature of her usual neat self. "I am the someone."

Vanessa inhaled. "What are we going to do? You think we could get Selena and her brother for murder?"

"Without evidence?" Addi snorted, "I doubt that. And if they are both working with the Ramirez family then the minute we open our mouth we would be toast."

"Yep." Vanessa nodded, "Joe would get rid of us, and he'd do it with pleasure. His sister lovingly calls him a psychopath. She can't get away with this."

Addi sighed. "She probably will."

"You mean we are going to stand by and watch her as she wins?" Vanessa asked hoarsely.

"What can we do?" Addi asked. "I had one run in with the Ramirez family, and I am telling you it wasn't pretty. I still have the rope burns to prove it. They are vicious. If they are still interested in me, I am as good as dead anyway if I open my mouth and start yapping about their friend Selena, tell me what do you think will happen to me?"

Addi whispered the last bit and tried not to panic. It was disheartening to learn that she wasn't as safe in Jamaica as she had thought.

"I could reset," Vanessa said in the silence. "Go back a couple of years. Warn Errol about Joe and Selena. Warn you about...what do you want me to warn you about?"

"Not to get involved with Devin Garcia. To be with Randy instead." Addi smiled. "It is a nice idea, Vanessa, but you only have the 't' in one palm. Maybe you are not a resetter."

"And maybe I am." Vanessa shrugged. "Just take me to a pathway, and we'll see."

"And if you don't go back and you can't reset?"

"Then I'll keep my mouth shut. Only tell Errol what I

know. Maybe he can wriggle out of this partnership with Selena."

Addi shook her head. "Then Selena would know something was up."

"I have to tell him, though," Vanessa said exasperation heavy in her voice. "He can't keep on doing business with these shady people and not know it, while Selena's sicko brother waits for him to mess up sometime."

Addi sighed. "Whatever you do or say, choose your words wisely. I like Errol but he is so stuck on Selena, he'd probably report this to her."

"No he wouldn't," Vanessa said confidently. "He would definitely not."

****

Vanessa still could not get Errol on the phone; she tried until nine o'clock and then finally went to his apartment fearing that Joe had gotten rid of him.

Errol's apartment was a good deal bigger and more luxurious than the one bedroom that she lived in. There was no sign of Errol, and there was no sign of forced entry.

She walked around feeling like a detective. She tried Errol's phone again and got the same voicemail message she had been getting for the past twenty-four hours. Finally, she went to the kitchen, and on the counter, she found a brochure, a phone charger, and a pack of gum.

The brochure advertised an open house by Burns and Daniels in Negril.

She exhaled in relief. It didn't take a genius to figure out that Errol must have gone to the open house yesterday, maybe stayed overnight. His phone charger was here which meant his phone battery was dead.

He usually called to check in when he stayed out overnight.

He had been doing that for the past four years. Vanessa was still not settled in her mind about it though, so she locked up the apartment and headed to the office. She wanted to talk to Errol. Maybe they could go somewhere and have breakfast.

She was stuck in traffic for a good half an hour, and when she reached the office building, she was beginning to question the wisdom of her actions. Why was she so jittery? Lack of sleep and a growing sense of paranoia had her in its grip.

She parked her car and spotted Errol's. Everything was good so far.

However, when she entered the office with the big Burns and Daniel's sign on the front door, she could sense that everything was not right. There was no one at the front desk. She walked past the reception desk and into the office area. Most of the staff were bundled around a door with a conference room sign on the door.

It didn't take a genius to figure out that there was pandemonium going on behind the door.

There was yelling. The employees didn't even acknowledge that there was a stranger in their midst.

She stood in the open office area and folded her arms and shook her head at their attitude and then she heard Errol's voice.

His was distinct.

"You have gone too far, Selena. When I said no business with this guy, I meant it! What's wrong with you?"

And then the conference door was yanked open, and Kenrick stepped out. "Selena, this is beneath me, I'll take my money where it is wanted. This guy is beyond offensive!"

Vanessa was holding herself, so tensely she didn't know if she could move if the roof decided to crash on her head.

Kenrick Douglas was here!

Her palms started sweating; no self-help book could have prepared her to face her rapist three years after the fact.

"Wait, Kenrick!" Selena was walking behind him, her high heels making click, click sounds on the tile. "Errol is just 50% of this business. He can't give arbitrary orders like this!"

He was heading in her direction. Vanessa's throat was dry— parchment dry.

Errol appeared at the door, his face beaded with sweat. "Take your business elsewhere you rapist!"

"For the love of all that is..." Selena looked back at Errol. "Shut the hell up!"

The staff made a collective gasp.

And Kenrick saw her at the same time.

He looked at her and then back at Errol and then he stopped.

"Oh," he laughed, "I remember you. What's your name again sweetie?

He clipped his fingers. "About three years ago, a party wasn't it? You took on me and the guys. Brave girl and sexy too. She was a trooper there were about six of us, I think."

He was talking to her. Bragging about how he defiled her.

Vanessa snapped out of her stupor, all the color had leached out of her face, but she still couldn't make her feet move.

"You told your boyfriend here that I raped you?" Kenrick's voice sounded like it was coming from a far tunnel.

"What are you doing here, Vanessa?" Selena interjected shrilly. "Can this day get any worse?"

Errol made a roaring sound, and before she knew it, Errol was hurling a chair at Kenrick Douglas' head.

Kenrick went down like an empty sack. Sprawled out on the floor, a gash on the side of his head, blood slowly making its snaking way along the tile crease.

"No!" Selena screamed. "No, no, no!"

"Somebody call the ambulance!" One of the employees screamed.

"It would be quicker if we take him to the hospital," someone else said.

Vanessa watched all of the commotion in a daze.

"You think he's dead?" Another asked.

"Come." She felt Errol's hands on her. She knew he helped her into his car. But everything felt like a blur after that.

****

Addi called Randy and told him that she'd be late.

"Don't bother leaving out," Randy said briskly. "Come upstairs. We can work together here. I have a meeting at eleven. You have your laptop?"

"Yes," Addi said, "Should I dress in office wear?"

"Jeans and t-shirt." Randy chuckled. "We are going to visit a site after this. Might as well."

Addi pulled her hair back in a ponytail, put on her jeans and a white t-shirt and was upstairs in a few minutes. She wished that more days could be like this.

Randy greeted her in similar attire; he had a cup of tea in his hands.

"Want some?"

"No thanks, I already had something." Addi settled herself at the dining room table. Randy already had the table half covered with a diagram.

"That's the next project," Randy said looking at the plan. "I am excited about this one. It's my own personal home."

Addi looked it over. "It seems so..."

"Huge?" Randy asked.

Addi glanced at him. He was freshly shaven this morning. He looked well rested. She was staring at him so long that he remarked on it.

"What? Is there something on my face or something?"

"No." Addi smiled. "I just like looking at you."

"Addi," Randy groaned. "Stop it!"

"Why, because Joe is threatening to kill me if you don't marry Selena?" Addi asked sweetly.

Randy stood stock-still. It was almost comical to watch. "How on earth...?"

"You won't believe this, but most of what..." Her phone buzzed, and Addi picked it up, "one second."

It was Errol, calling from Vanessa's phone.

"Addi, you at work?"

"Yes. Not at Royalty Insurance, though. At Randy's place."

"This is going to be an imposition." Errol sounded panicked, "but Vanessa came to the office today and saw Kenrick Douglas. I may have just killed him. She is almost catatonic. I need someone to look out for her. Can I take her up there?"

"Sure." Addi looked at Randy, "well let me ask..."

She asked Randy who had a confused look on his face. "Okay."

He frowned at her. "What's going on?"

"Vanessa lives three doors down from my place. She is the one who told me about the threat and many other things. You may need to sit down for this. She is coming up with Errol."

It wasn't long before they were all seated in the living room. Errol was jittery and twitching, Vanessa huddled in a corner of the settee, and she wasn't talking.

Errol soon explained why.

"I am going to have to turn myself in to the police," Errol said his voice high pitched. He kept wiping his face with a damp looking kerchief. "I don't know why I threw that chair. I am not a violent man, but you should have seen his sneer. He couldn't even remember her name!"

"Okay, calm down," Randy said. "Maybe I should call Selena find out if he is dead."

"No!" Addi shook her head vigorously. "Don't call her."

It was her time to talk. She told them exactly what Vanessa had said to her earlier that morning.

The entire room went silent.

Errol was shaking his head like he was trying to dislodge something from his ear and Randy was gripping the arm of the chair like a man hanging on for dear life.

"Cassius Green? Royalty Insurance? No." Randy was having trouble adjusting to the news too.

"The Ramirez, crime family?" Errol muttered. "I wondered why those deals were so easy to clinch. Why we didn't have competition with other real estate places, why Selena had suddenly become so nice to me that time couple years ago..." he bit his lip.

"I should travel," Vanessa said hoarsely while the men digested the information.

"Vanessa?" They all turned to her.

"What is she talking about?" Randy whispered as if Vanessa wasn't right there.

"Time travel," Addi said. "She is a half resetter or something like that."

Chapter Eighteen

"This is madness," Errol muttered. "I should be handing myself over to the police now. I shouldn't be going to Mandeville to find some rock called a pathway to test out this stupid theory. I can't believe that you believe this, Randy."

Randy glanced over at Addi who was sitting in the passenger side of the car. "I believe it, and what's more, I endorse it. Addi didn't have to tell me twice to get going."

"And what if it doesn't work?" Errol asked his voice trembled when he said work.

"Then we find another resetter," Vanessa said, she was regaining her energy the farther they drove from Montego Bay. "Now that I know about them, I have to change my past."

"Oh, so resetters are easy to find like that?" Errol clipped his fingers. "I thought a 't' in your palms was something that was scarce as hen's teeth."

"They aren't easy to find," Addi muttered. "Not easy at

all."

"When would you go back to, Vanessa?" Randy looked in the rearview mirror at her.

"Definitely before Kenrick Douglas put his stinky fingers on my life," Vanessa said, "August 1999 was a good year. Errol was my friend and client. I was working at Crowns Gym. My bosses were great. I had a nice flat, nothing like your place Randy but I guess when I go back to '99 there will be no Primrose Apartments."

"No." Randy shook his head. "Errol sold me that land in late 2000."

"And he met Selena," Errol said wistfully. "After Addi rejected him."

"That will not happen." Addi curled her fingers through Randy's. "If I get the chance to do it all again, I am going to tell my younger self that it is now or never."

"There are so many wrongs to set right," Randy murmured. "So many mistakes. How will Vanessa do it? She'll be a stranger to us, and how will she stop Joe? He can't be allowed to run unchecked."

"If any of this is even remotely possible. I know a way to get Joe off the streets." Errol mumbled. "I can't believe that I am participating in this fantasy."

"How will you get him off the streets?" Vanessa asked softly.

Errol closed his eyes and then grunted. "They had him on videotape in March 1999. He was with a crony of his in a shoplifting sting of some Chinese retailers downtown. I was the one who paid off the police to look the other way because Selena begged me to."

"You?" Addi turned around and gave Errol a harsh stare. "You were whipped."

"I was." Errol laughed mirthlessly. "I had a hand in creating the monster that is Joe."

"And Selena?" Vanessa asked, "what will you do about her?"

"Cut ties!" Errol growled. "End our partnership. Three years ago if I did that she'd be shocked. Back then I thought the sun rose and set on her. Without Joe, I guess she wouldn't be able to accomplish most of her evil deeds. I'd also warn her about her business connections with the Ramirez family, scare her a little. Deep down she is not a bad person. Joe is the evil that keeps on giving."

"I don't know about that charitable view of her but what you said sounds like a plan." Vanessa was warming up to the idea of having a do-over.

Addi wanted to caution her to curb her enthusiasm. There was no guarantee, here.

"And you Addi?" Vanessa asked, "what will you do about your gangster fiancé?"

"Run as far away in the opposite direction as I can," Addi muttered. "He wasn't even a fiancé, just a guy I was talking to for three months. Exploring the possibilities of having a relationship without Randy and proving to myself that I could."

Randy snorted.

"And Randy?" Vanessa chuckled. "What will you do?"

"Find Addi, marry her as soon as it can be arranged and have a full month honeymoon in a little cottage in Negril."

They all chuckled at that.

But the closer they got to Mandeville and to Addi's old house, the more solemn everyone became.

"We should stop for stationery," Randy said when they reached the town of Mandeville. "I think we should each write to ourselves; you know personal letters. In case there is skepticism. Addi carried back a book with her from the future when she went back to 1995."

"Good idea, though that book was basically worthless to Sky because she had used the wrong ink." Addi clipped her fingers. "I have a notepad and pens in my bag. No need to stop."

"I am just hoping that this works," Errol muttered, "because if not, I am going to be somebody's girlfriend in jail."

****

When they drove up to Addi's place, there was nobody home. It was the middle of a workday anyway; her parents would be at work.

Addi rummaged in her bag for her notepad. She tore off a page for each of them. She only found two pens. She handed one to Errol and one to Randy. "Guys first."

Errol grunted. "What should I tell my past-clueless-self about the future? Should I address it as, 'Hi idiot you are wasting away your life loving a woman who is not worth it, who is about to get in bed with the mafia.'"

Randy looked between him and Vanessa. "Maybe you should leave a note to yourself that you should pay attention to one particular woman who is closer to home."

Errol squirmed.

Vanessa raised an eyebrow and then looked at Errol. "That would be a good idea."

"You would date me?" Errol asked, "really?"

"Yes. Why not? You are a special guy, Errol. I liked you in '99, but all you did was talk about Selena."

Errol looked like he would faint.

Randy's phone rang. And he glanced at the call display. It was Selena.

"Selena everybody," he muttered.

He answered while everybody stayed silent and tense.

"Randy, where are you?" Selena asked sourly. "I had the kind of day you wouldn't believe."

"I am doing some business in Mandeville," Randy said. "What's up?"

"Errol went all caveman and assaulted Kenrick Douglas in the office."

"Is Kenrick okay?" Randy asked.

"Yes he is, but he has a terrible headache, and he needed six stitches for the gash on his face. I convinced him not to press charges against Errol though. So all is well on that front."

"When are you coming back home?" Selena asked. "I need some sanity restored to my world. I need you, Randy."

"Selena," Randy asked tensely, "did you tell your brother to poison Cassius Green because you wanted me to have that insurance company?"

"No!" Selena gasped.

"Are you doing business with the Ramirez family?"

"No!" Selena was practically shouting.

"Did you know that Joe threatened to kill Addi if I didn't marry you?"

"Where are you getting all of this nonsense from?" Selena sounded out of breath. "This is pure garbage."

"It's over, Selena," Randy said tersely. "I can't trust you anymore. I am not even sure I know you."

"You can't break up with me!" Selena screeched, "not like this, especially about stuff that I didn't do, stuff that you can't prove. If you think that you are going to leave me for Addison Porter, you have another think coming. I'll make sure that neither of you ever live a happy day together. You mark my words."

She crashed down the phone into Randy's ear.

"That was loud," Vanessa said. "I could hear her all the way from the backseat."

"If this doesn't work, I just made things very difficult for our current life." Randy turned to Addi. "I am happy I did it though. I can't live without you, Magnet, fighting it is useless."

Addi smiled. "Maybe we should stay and face whatever Joe and Selena have in store for us."

"Ahem." Vanessa poked her head between the two of them. "I need to reset, desperately. I was the one who was gang-raped."

"How is Kenrick?" Errol looked up from his letter.

"Alive and feeling generous toward you because of Selena," Randy said. "No charges will be pressed."

"More's the pity," Errol said. "I was liking the idea of being a fugitive running from the law."

Vanessa sighed. "How does this work, Addi?"

"You think of the year that you want to go back to and the date. Place your hand with the 't' on the rock, and then you will end up there."

"Okay." Vanessa inhaled. "Hurry up your notes. I want to get this show on the road."

They wrote short letters to their unsuspecting past selves and handed them to Vanessa.

"Find us in July 16, 2000. I wrote down directions to the Jefferson house. Sky and Travis are getting married. Don't be disappointed if this doesn't happen," Addi cautioned. "We can make do with the present. It's not going to be easy but we can..."

Vanessa wasn't listening she stepped toward the rock, placed her hand with the notes in it and closed her eyes.

Chapter Nineteen

Skyler's Wedding- July 2000

"So we meet again, Addi."

Addi knew it was Randy even before she turned around. She had been aware of him through the whole service and then the reception. In a room full of good-looking men he was a standout. She was sure that she was not the only female who was ogling him.

She turned around slowly from where she was to take him in fully and then just like that her once steady hands started to tremble on the glass of wine.

"Randy didn't see you there." She was trying for nonchalant. She failed.

"Liar." Randy laughed. "It was a nice wedding. You made a beautiful maid of honor."

"Thanks." Addi nodded. "I almost didn't show up. Sky and Travis were crazy enough to plan a large wedding in a mere two weeks."

"But you did come. It's nice to see you again." Randy cleared his throat. "Can we go somewhere quiet and talk?" He looked around the crowded poolside of the Jefferson mansion. "Maybe to the gardens?"

Addi bit her lip and then shook her head. "I don't think so. I meant what I said, Randy. I can't have a relationship with you."

"Yes, I remember," Randy nodded, "Oh I remember last year in New York. You said I was a past mistake and that I had no place in your life this time around."

"That's right." Addi nodded. "I am glad you got the message."

"I did." Randy shrugged. "I just don't get the reason for the message."

Addi put the drink on a table and then turned around again. "Okay, come on."

Randy raised an eyebrow but did not argue. He followed her as she headed down a cobbled stone walkway all the way to a mini bridge where there was a pond and an unoccupied gazebo.

It was quite picturesque. There were koi in the pond—little colorful bodies glinting in the six o'clock sunlight. Addi stood in the gazebo her hands braced on the railing, her long curly hair in a half up half down hairdo. Her filmy long pink dress floated around her. She looked like a princess waiting for her loyal subject.

"Can I take your picture?" He asked taking out his camera, "this is too lovely a moment not to capture."

Addi seemed like she thought about it for a moment and then she nodded. "Go ahead."

He snapped several shots of her and then smiled. "I guess you are used to this and all, you being a model."

"That was last year." Addi sat in one of the chairs in the gazebo. "This year I am writing a novel."

"That's quite a departure from what you said you were doing before." Randy stepped up into the gazebo and sat before her.

He loosened his bow tie and raised an eyebrow. "In the previous time, you were a doctor in sociology. You should be pursuing a masters degree by now."

"You remembered that?" Addi asked flippantly.

"I remember everything you ever told me." Randy leaned forward and frowned. "I invested in those tech stocks you told me about."

"Good for you." Addi smiled at him, the first genuine smile he was seeing from her in a while.

"I invested some of my money in real estate. After the 96 meltdown, for cheap."

"And where are you working now, or are you just investing? Addi asked him.

Interest. Finally.

Randy relaxed somewhat. "I am working at Gordon and Fletcher, chief accounting officer for their telecommunications company. That's the reason I was at the tech summit last year in New York."

"That sounds great," Addi looked at him and then away, "really great."

"I am still not married to any pastor's daughter or have any hopes of joining the ministry." Randy reminded her of what she had told him that he had ended up doing before she had reset things.

"I am very much interested in knowing why we can't be together. You have written me off based on previous information from a timeline that I am not privy to."

Addi sighed. "I don't remember much of what happened.

I have this book where I wrote down stuff, and I cautioned myself never to get involved with you."

Randy leaned back in the chair and rubbed the back of his neck. "This is frustrating Addison. You and I have chemistry. It is stupid for us not to explore that in the here and now. I am single. You are single. I have liked you since you were a kid. Now you are a grown, gorgeous woman. You have to give us a chance."

"No!" Addi stood up. "I have other plans."

"You have a boyfriend?" Randy asked belatedly.

"Yes." Addison nodded. "The timing for us is just off."

"I'd say." Randy huffed. "I don't know why I assumed you were single. Josh never mentioned to me that you were dating."

He got up and stood beside her, looking down in the fishpond. "I guess we aren't meant to be after all."

"I guess so." Addi looked at him, and her lips had a slight tremor. "I am going back to the party."

"You can break it off with him," Randy said holding her hand. "I'll wait."

Addi looked down at their joined hands and then up at Randy. The pulse in her palm was racing, and she knew her voice would be breathless. "I don't think I should."

"You should." Randy leaned toward her so close she could feel the heat from his face. She could feel his breath on her skin. "When you do, call me."

Addi inhaled tremulously and then stepped away from him. "I don't think so. Goodbye Randy."

"Never goodbye," Randy gave her a bitter half-smile, "not between you and me. I have a feeling we were meant to be together..."

"Dream on," Addi said heading back to the reception. Sky would be having the tossing of the bouquet; maybe she could catch it, as handsome as Randy was, as right as it felt when she looked at him, there had to be someone else out there.

She looked behind at him leaning on the column of the gazebo. His eyes looked sad as if he were compelling her to come back.

She shrugged off the feeling that she should turn back to him and talk. She didn't want her life to be stuck in a time warp. Surely, Randy was not the only guy in the world for her. Devin Garcia was shaping up to be a good candidate for romance, and he was a respectable preacher too.

"Excuse me." She bumped into a girl. She had a faint resemblance to Sky. Her hair was in a stylish topknot.

The girl looked at Addi and then put her hand on her heart in relief. "I almost missed the party and you."

"Me?" Addi squeaked. She had never seen this girl before.

"Yes, you." the girl giggled. "This is a really lovely place." She looked around and then saw Randy.

"Randy looks unhappy."

"Who are you?" Addi asked frowning.

"Oh, sorry." She held out her hand to be shaken. "My name is Vanessa Rochester Daniels."

"I am Addison Porter." Addi shook her hand.

"I know." Vanessa smiled. "I have this for you."

She handed Addi an envelope.

"I have one for Randy as well."

Vanessa walked over to Randy and handed him a similar envelope.

"If you guys want to talk, I am staying at the Pegasus with my husband." She touched Addi's arm. "We'll be there for three days. Oh, and here's my number just in case."

She handed Addi a business card.

Addi fanned the envelope distrustfully. "What's this about?"

"I have no clue. I never read it." Vanessa walked away and disappeared into the crowd.

Addi headed back to the gazebo where Randy was.

He was already reading his note, a frown on his face.

She tore open hers and sat down on one of the benches with a thud. This was her handwriting. All the loops and curvatures were distinctly hers.

Dear Addi,

There is not a lot of space on this sheet of paper and not a lot of time to write this. Vanessa will explain everything to you. What you need to know right now is that Devin Garcia is a criminal and is in bed with the mafia. You are to break it off with him now. Secondly, Randy is the guy for you. You'll always love him. This is your chance to have a happy ever after with Randy, don't screw it up. Now or Never, Addi. Now or Never.

Randy sat down beside her and shook his head. "I can't believe this..."

"What does yours say?" Addi whispered.

Randy took out the letter and read it with a frown.

Dear Randy,

Addi rejected you? So what? You are going to pursue her until she cracks. You love her; you'll never quite capture this feeling with anybody but her, trust me. That guy, Garcia that she is calling her boyfriend is nothing but a criminal and will create a lot of strife in her life in a couple of years. You can't let her go now. She is your magnet, don't fight it.

Addi gasped and looked at Randy.

"Read yours," Randy said hoarsely.

She did.

Randy was silent after that.

"That girl, Vanessa, is a resetter," Addi said after a while.

"Or a very clever forger who can duplicate our handwriting."

Randy smirked, "I wonder what on earth we did to mess up our lives after this?"

"Who knows?" Addi said faintly.

"Your boyfriend is a criminal?" Randy laughed softly. "This is the guy you were going to turn me down for. That's disgraceful."

"He's not my boyfriend yet!" Addi protested. "Well, not really. I can't believe that he is a criminal. He is a pastor at his church, a fine upstanding citizen. I doubt the veracity of this letter."

She looked at it again. "Maybe somebody is playing a trick on us."

"A mafia pastor?" Randy whistled. "What is this world coming to?"

"This is crazy." Addi got up. "I am going to call Devin right now and ask him if it's true."

"No, you are not," Randy said solemnly. "You are going to break it off with him without any explanation, tell him you met the guy you were destined to marry."

Addi snorted. "Stop being ridiculous, Randy. I can't get a letter to myself out of nowhere and not question it. Besides, I am not sure I want to just break up with Devin, and what's more, you can't make me."

"Oh yes I can make you," Randy said aggressively. "If I have to trail you for the next couple of days if I have to beg and plead with you for the next couple of months, or years. That's what I am going to do.

"You are going to throw away that stupid future book in which you have written all sorts of nonsense about me, and you are going to choose me because Addi, I am choosing you. This time, this place, this hour. I am choosing you. Consider me your shadow until you choose me too."

"You are scaring me with your macho man talk." Addi got

up. "I am going to get to the bottom of this. I'll find this Vanessa person and hear her explanation."

Randy got up and stared at her. "I am coming with you. For the record, this could have ended so much different right now if you weren't such a stubborn infuriating female."

"How would you like it to end?" Addi asked.

Randy grabbed her hand and folded it into his. "I was hoping that you would take your own advice, the most recent one that is, and realize that for you and me, this is now or never."

"But I can do better," Addi whispered. "I already spent twenty years with you in another lifetime, and you married someone else. I was never first. I was your secret lover, your dirty little secret while you carried on with your life."

"And I am asking you to forget that," Randy pulled her closer. "You just admitted in your letter that you would always love me. There is no doing better for either of us, darling. We always find our way back to each other one way or the other. At this moment I wish you would allow us the chance to start afresh, to reset, properly this time. "

"I don't know..." Addi still resisted.

Randy swore under his breath. "Now I understand why I walked away before, but not this time, Missy. This time, I am sticking to you like glue."

He bent his head until their noses were touching. "Addi, stop fighting us."

Addi swallowed nervously. "But I..."

She slumped her shoulders. "Randy I am scared. Suppose we don't last, suppose I get hurt, suppose life doesn't end up the way that we want, suppose...."

Randy kissed away her litany of suppositions and then whispered. "Suppose we are happy, suppose we grow old together, suppose we put away the fear and embrace the love."

"Okay," Addi whispered, "I hear you."

Chapter Twenty

The day after the reception they arranged to meet Vanessa and her husband at the Pegasus for lunch, Randy's workplace was pretty close by, but Addi was running late. Sky was the one who woke her up.

"I approve." Sky squealed gleefully in her ear, "I can now enjoy my honeymoon knowing that you are on the right path."

"What are you talking about?" Addi husked and then looked at the clock on the side table.

"You and Randy. I saw you two by the gazebo." Sky chuckled. "Call me when you get up properly."

Addi jumped up after hanging up the phone. She had barely slept a wink the night before, she and Randy had stayed up talking until the early hours. They had a lot of catching up to do.

Randy was in the middle of launching out on his own business ventures, and she still had a couple of modeling gigs to do that summer. Sometime in the middle of the night, she had, on the spur of the moment, agreed to move back to Jamaica.

The post-reception cleanup crew was almost done when Randy left.

She rushed to bathe and get dressed. It took her a couple of minutes to leave the house though. Mrs. Jefferson insisted that she have a cup of tea with her and then she had to drive Sky's car down the hill slowly. She heaved a sigh of relief when she reached the hotel. She had taken the wrong road more than once.

They were at the poolside dining room. She spotted Randy first; he waved her over to the table. Vanessa and a hulking muscular guy who she introduced as her husband Errol was with him.

"I am a realtor," Errol said when she sat down. "I was just telling Randy that Vanessa suggested I sell him a particular property that's just on the market because he bought it in the future."

"Really?" Addi smiled and then looked between the two of them. "I am so curious, what's the story here? I mean, it's not everyday one gets a note from their future self."

"It's Vanessa's story to tell," Errol said pointing to his wife. "I was quite taken aback by the whole thing too. I sent myself a letter too. It seems as if I was a part of the whole scenario that led to Van resetting things."

"His reaction was priceless when I handed him the note..." Vanessa giggled, "You see, I was Errol's personal trainer, and he had a partnership in a real estate firm, Daniels and Burns. Have you ever heard of it?"

"No." Addi shook her head.

Randy frowned. "Maybe. The name rings a bell. I may have."

"The company is now defunct." Errol shrugged. "It is just Errol Daniels Realtor now."

"Well, you see what happened was," Vanessa laughed. "Randy was engaged to Selena Burns, Errol's business partner.

"Errol had a serious case of infatuation with her and Addi here worked for you and I had an unfortunate run-in with a basketball player."

"What?" Addi frowned, "I worked for Randy?"

"Yes." Vanessa nodded. "As his personal assistant."

Addi looked at Randy and chuckled. "Really now? I wonder if I got any work done."

"I am sure you did." Vanessa looked as if she was enjoying herself. "You didn't work for him for a long time though. You discovered that one of my palms had a 't' and we sort of had our reasons for coming back and one thing led to another. I went to your place Addi in Mandeville with the stone. And you all gave me your notes.

"I went back to August '99. There was a party I had to avoid, some friends I had to ditch and Errol, I had to convince him of the whole time travel thing. He eventually came around."

Errol smiled. "I did come around. Though sometimes, it is a bit hard to digest. I left the partnership with Selena that same year, went out on my own, lost the weight the following year and then asked Vanessa to marry me."

Addi smiled. "How sweet."

"Thank you, Addi," Vanessa said spontaneously, "because of you, a very bad guy is behind bars. You ever heard of Joe Burns?"

"No." Addi shook her head.

"Well, he was a feature in your future. Now he won't be."

"Same surname as this Selena person?" Randy asked interestedly.

"Yes, her twin brother. He was caught on tape doing a whole host of bad stuff. He'll be in prison for a while."

"And Selena, where is she now?" Addi asked.

"Married." Vanessa grinned. "To Kenrick Douglas, ever heard of him?"

"Yes." Addi nodded, "basketball player."

"They are the perfect match I think." Vanessa chuckled. "Errol thinks that they won't last, but I think they will. Selena convinced Kenrick not to sign a prenup. That will keep him in line for a while."

Addi was not as interested in this Selena person or their stories. She liked Vanessa though, and she exchanged numbers with her. She had never heard of a half resetter and wanted to explore more of what that meant.

Randy and Errol exchanged business cards and then the other couple left to make another appointment. Addi and Randy were alone.

Addi felt pensive.

"Pinch me. I need to make sure that I am not dreaming." Addi held out her hand.

"I'll never hurt you." Randy kissed her palm instead. "You are not dreaming, you are here with me, and we are finally going to make you, and I happen."

He leaned across the table and whispered. "Addi will you marry me?"

"Yes." Addi smiled, her eyes filled with hope for the future. "Forever, yes!"

The End

Author's Notes

Dear Reader,

Many thanks for sticking with the series so far. When I wrote, **Never Too Late**, Randy was married and Addi was his mistress for twenty years and I was toying with the idea of giving Addi a different love interest after her reset.

After all, she should have a happily ever after with someone who had not broken her heart. But... Randy said no, and I tend to listen to my characters. It makes the writing easier. I hope you liked this book and the outcome.

The last book in the series is, **Almost Never**. Josh gets his own story with a convict! The excerpt is on the next page.

As usual, thank you for reading.

Thanks again. All the best,

Brenda

Here is an excerpt from Almost Never

Fort Augusta Adult Correctional Center, Jamaica, January 2017

"If you could change one thing about your life what would it be?" Portia read the question out loud to her cellmates, and they laughed heartily.

"My pen pal is an idiot!" she snorted. "How can you ask a woman in prison what she would change? Getting put in prison of course."

She made a face at the letter and then continued reading. *"I would like to know more about you. I know this our third letter to each other, but I hardly know a thing about you. You've been very vague. Is your name Honey Pee Gordon and are you really just nineteen years old? You write with a maturity far beyond your years."*

"Honey Pee?" Inga asked in her heavy German accent. "That sounds gross."

"It was the best that I could come up with," Portia snorted. "If I told my pen pal my real name, they would go and research stuff on me, and then I would have no pen pal."

"I like this lady. She sounds nice. Her letters are something to look forward to in this hellhole. Whenever you heifers leave, you always promise to write and I never hear back from any of you."

"You know you wouldn't write us back either," Janet said squinting over her glasses. "When you leave here, you try to forget that you were ever in this situation and that means you forget some of the friends you have made here. It's just life."

Janet was a teacher who had been caught trying to smuggle cocaine through the airport for her boyfriend. Through the years more persons like her were added to the prison population. Couple years ago they had a cellmate who was a lawyer. She had stolen from her clients.

"I'll remember you, Honey Pee," Inga said gutturally. "But writing you, I don't know about that. I didn't even know people still write to each other with pen and paper. You know that there is a thing called the Internet?"

"Of course she does," Hailey smirked. "She has not been in here that long."

"Yes, I have been in here a long time—twelve years," Portia said sarcastically. "This January makes twelve wonderful years of Fort Augusta hospitality."

The rest of the girls laughed because there was nothing wonderful about Fort Augusta and none of them would be staying in there for that length of time.

Of the twelve of them who were jammed in the cell, Portia was probably the only one who had not been a drug mule. She was there the longest. She had a sort of seniority among them.

She had been housed in Fort Augusta from she was little more than a girl. An oversight by the state that had never been corrected because she had nobody to lobby on her behalf.

No family.

No friends.

One year a children's advocate had taken up her cause, but then she had turned eighteen and had lost the little veneer of sympathy that she might have gotten from some segments of society.

After all, she was the girl who had sent a collective gasp of horror reeling through the country after her crime. She was the girl who had lawmakers calling for the resumption of capital punishment and churchgoers, especially from her father's flock, asking for her head on a stick.

"Hey, Honey Pee." Janet snapped her fingers. "Tell us about your pen pal."

Portia snapped out of her reverie and took up the letter. It was on good quality paper, and the handwriting was very pretty.

"My pen pal is a grandmother of four. She is recently retired and has a lot of time on her hands. She says her women's group decided to do something different for a change and they decided to mentor women in prison through the pen pal program."

Portia shrugged. "I think it is a great idea."

"Yeah, brilliant," Inga snorted. "Why didn't I get a letter from one of these charitable ladies?"

"Because you will get out soon. I think they correspond with people who are going to be here for a long time."

"I have a pen pal." Janet rolled her eyes. "She writes me pages and pages of scripture. I had to tell her to stop. It feels like we have church services here every day. I think she is missing the point of the whole pen pal thing."

Portia nodded. "My pen pal is trying to include me in her life. She tells me stuff about herself, like the fact that she has two adult children. Her daughter is an interior decorator and has three children.

"Her son is a hotshot businessman who is currently single and has no plans to get married. They had a family reunion the other day, and she served her signature dish—bread pudding and vanilla ice cream."

"And yet you hide your real name from her." Inga snorted. "Tell her the truth and let the friendship be more honest."

"I might." Portia shrugged. "One day."

She picked up the letter and looked at her pen pal's name, *Victoria Porter*.

Portia wondered if she would ever hear from Victoria again

if she told her her real name and her real situation.

Or would she drive such horror in the poor lady that her lone contact with the outside world would cease writing her?

OTHER BOOKS BY BRENDA BARRETT

Wiley Brothers Series

Between Brothers (Book 0)- The beginning of the Wiley brothers saga, Joseph Wiley's unconventional family life may prove to be fatal to some members of the family.

For Pete's Sake (Book 1)- Preston has a run in with a child named Pete who claims that he is the grandson of their former housekeeper Pamela Stone.

Crossing Jordan (Book 2)- Jordan is miffed when Shawn takes her new fiancé to Jamaica and insists that he be best man at their wedding.

Fire and Walter (Book 3)- Walter's shady past is affecting his new appointment as church elder. The situation would not only compromise him but a particular newly married church sister as well.

The Perfect Guy (Book 4) - Guy decides to explore the world of farming, becomes an apprentice to a farmer and lives a humble life. He is constantly rebuffed by the woman that he loves because she thinks he is poor!

The Patience of A Saint (Book 5)- Saint attends his own divorce party put on by his soon to be ex wife and they end up complicating matters.

A Case of Love (Book 6)- Case unwittingly buys a bride from a human trafficking ring a few days before his own wedding.

Resetter Series

Never Too Late (Book 1)- Addi finds out she is a resetter and goes back to the summer of 92 to change her family's lives.

Never Say Never (Book 2)- Skyler's handsome college lecturer, who happens to be her neighbor, has a 't' in his palms. Should she tell him the significance of it. If she does, would he believe her?

Now or Never (Book 3)- Ten years later Addi and Randy meet again at Randy's engagement party. Why is it that the chemistry between them was still so potent? Can they ever have a future together? Would Randy choose her this time around?

Almost Never (Book 4)- Tech genius Joshua Porter had all but given up on love. He then meets Portia, an inmate at the female penitentiary and his life takes a turn for the adventurous.

The Scarlett Family Series

Scarlett Baby (Book 1)- When the head of the Scarlett family died, Yuri had to return home to Treasure Beach for the funeral. What he didn't count on was seeing Marla, his childhood sweetheart and his best friend's wife. And when emotions overwhelm them and a few months later Marla is pregnant, Yuri wants the impossible: his best friend's wife and the baby they made together...

Scarlett Sinner (Book 2)- Pastor Troy Scarlett realizes the hard way that some sins are bound to be revealed, like the child that he had out of wedlock with his wife's mortal enemy from college. His wife Chelsea was not happy with the status quo. She was not taking care of the son of the woman she had so despised from college. And she could not get over the deep betrayal that she felt from her husband's indiscretion.

Scarlett Secret (Book 3)- Terri Scarlett had a soft spot for her friend, Lola. She was funny and sweet and they looked remarkably alike. But when Lola's Arab prince demands his bride, Terri foolishly exchange places with her friend and they meet up on a world of trouble.

Scarlett Love (Book 4)- Slater always looked forward to delivering packages to the law firm where he could get a glimpse of the stunning female lawyer, Amoy Gardener. Unfortunately, for Slater a woman like Amoy would not take him seriously, especially when she found out that he could not read!

Scarlett Promise (Book 5)- Driven by desperation Lisa Barclay decides to make some extra money by prostituting herself after being kicked out in the streets. Her first customer turns out to be a popular government senator and then to her horror he dies...

Scarlett Bride (Book 6)- When Oliver Scarlett's missionary work in the Congo region was coming to an end, he had a decision to make, marry Ashaki Azanga and save her from being the fourth wife to the chief of the village or leave her to her fate and get on with his life...

Scarlett Heart (Book 7)- After receiving a heart transplant shy librarian Noah Scarlett started to take on character traits that were unlike him and he kept dreaming of a girl named Cassandra Green...

Rebound Series

On The Rebound- For Better or Worse, Brandon vowed to stay with Ashley, but when worse got too much he moved out and met Nadine. For the first time in years he felt happy, but then Ashley remembered her wedding vows...

On The Rebound 2- Ashley reinvented herself and was now a first lady in a country church in Primrose Hill, but her obsessed ex friend Regina showed up and started digging into the lives of the saints at church. Somebody didn't like Regina's digging. Someone had secrets that were shocking enough to kill for...

Magnolia Sisters

Dear Mystery Guy (Book 1)- Della Gold details her life in a journal dedicated to a mystery guy. But when fascination turns into obsession she finds herself wanting to learn even more about him but in her pursuit of the mystery guy she begins to learn more about herself...

Bad Girl Blues (Book 2)- Brigid Manderson wanted to go to med school but for the time being she was an escort working for her mother, an ex-prostitute. When her latest customer offers her the opportunity of a lifetime would she take it? Or would she choose the harder path and uncertain love with a Christian guy?

Her Mistaken Dreams (Book 3)- Caitlin Denvers dream guy had serious issues. He has a dead wife in his past and he was the main suspect in her murder. Did he really do it? Or did Caitlin for the first time have a mistaken dream?

Just Like Yesterday (Book 4)- Hazel Brown lost six months of memory including the summer that she conceived her son, and had no idea who his father could be. Now that she had the means to fight to get him back from the Deckers, she finds out that the handsome Curtis Decker is willing to share her son with her after all.

New Song Series

Going Solo (Book 1)- Carson Bell, had a lovely voice, a heart of gold, and was no slouch in the looks department. So why did Alice abandon him and their daughter? What did she want after ten years of silence?

Duet on Fire (Book 2)- Ian and Ruby had problems trying to conceive a child. If that wasn't enough, her ex-lover the current pastor of their church wants her back...

Tangled Chords (Book 3)- Xavier Bell, the poor, ugly duckling has made it rich and his looks have been incredibly improved too. Farrah Knight, hotel heiress had cruelly rejected him in the past but now she needed help. Could Xavier forgive and forget?

Broken Harmony(Book 4)- Aaron Lee, wanted the top job in his family company but he had a moral clause to consider just when Alka, his married ex-girlfriend walks back into his life.

A Past Refrain (Book 5)- Jayce had issues with forgetting Haley Greenwald even though he had a new woman in his life. Will he ever be able to shake his love for Haley?

Perfect Melody (Book 6)- Logan Moore had the perfect wife, Melody but his secretary Sabrina was hell bent on breaking up the family. Sabrina wanted Logan whatever the cost and she had a secret about Melody, that could shatter Melody's image to everyone.

The Bancroft Family Series

Homely Girl (Book 0) - April and Taj were opposites in so many ways. He was the cute, athletic boy that everybody wanted to be friends with. She was the overweight, shy, and withdrawn girl. Do April and Taj have a love that can last a lifetime? Or will time and separate paths rip them apart?

Saving Face (Book 1) - Mount Faith University drama begins with a dead president and several suspects including the president in waiting Ryan Bancroft.

Tattered Tiara (Book 2) - Micah Bancroft is targeted by femme fatale Deidra Durkheim. There are also several rape cases to be solved.

Private Dancer (Book 3) Adrian Bancroft was gutted when he returned to Jamaica and found out that his first and only love Cathy Taylor was a stripper and was literally owned by the menacing drug lord, Nanjo Jones.

Goodbye Lonely (Book 4) - Kylie Bancroft was shy and had to resort to going to confidence classes. How could she win the love of Gareth Beecher, her faculty adviser, a man with a jealous ex-wife in his past and a current mystery surrounding a hand found in his garden?

Practice Run (Book 5) - Marcus Bancroft had many reasons to avoid Mount Faith but Deidra Durkheim was not one of them. Unfortunately, on one of his visits he was the victim of a deliberate hit and run.

Sense of Rumor (Book 6) - Arnella Bancroft was the wild, passionate Bancroft, the creative loner who didn't mind living dangerously; but when a terrible thing happened to her at her friend Tracy's party, it changed her. She found that courting rumors can be devastating and that only the truth could set her free.

A Younger Man (Book 7) - Pastor Vanley Bancroft loved Anita Parkinson despite their fifteen-year age gap, but Anita had a secret, one that she could not reveal to Vanley. To tell him would change his feelings toward her, or force him to give up the ministry that he loved so much.

Just To See Her (Book 8) - Jessica Bancroft had the opportunity to meet her fantasy guy Khaled, he was finally coming to Mount Faith but she had feelings for Clay Reid, a guy who had all the qualities she was looking for. Who would she choose and what about the weird fascination Khaled had for Clay?

The Three Rivers Series

Private Sins (Book 1)- Kelly, the first lady at Three Rivers Church was pregnant for the first elder of her church. Could she keep the secret from her husband and pretend that all was well?

Loving Mr. Wright (Book 2)- Erica saw one last opportunity to ditch her single life when Caleb Wright appeared in her town. He was perfect for her, but what was he hiding?

Unholy Matrimony (Book 3) - Phoebe had a problem, she was poor and unhappy. Her solution to marry a rich man was derailed along the way with her feelings for Charles Black, the poor guy next door.

If It Ain't Broke (Book 4)- Chris Donahue wanted a place in his child's life. Pinky Black just wanted his love. She also wanted him to forget his obsession with Kelly and love her. That shouldn't be so hard? Should it?

Contemporary Romance/Drama

*After The End--*Torn between two lovers. Colleen married her high school sweetheart, Isaiah, hoping that they would live happily ever after but life intruded and Isaiah disappeared at sea. She found work with the rich and handsome, Enrique Lopez, as a housekeeper and realized that she couldn't keep him at arms length...

Love Triangle: Three Sides To The Story- George, the husband, Marie, the wife and Karen-the mistress. They all get to tell their side of the story.

The Preacher And The Prostitute - Prostitution and the

clergy don't mix. Tell that to ex-prostitute, Maribel, who finds herself in love with the Pastor at her church. Can an ex-prostitute and a pastor have a future together?

New Beginnings - Inner city girl Geneva was offered an opportunity of a lifetime when she found out that her 'real' father was a very wealthy man. Her decision to live up-town meant that she had to leave Froggie, her 'ghetto don,' behind. She also found herself battling with her stepmother and battling her emotions for Justin, a suave up-towner.

Full Circle- After graduating from university, Diana wanted to return to Jamaica to find her siblings. What she didn't foresee was that she would meet Robert Cassidy and that both their pasts would be intertwined, and that disturbing questions would pop up about their parentage, just when they were getting close.

Historical Fiction/Romance

The Empty Hammock- Workaholic, Ana Mendez, fell asleep in a hammock and woke up in the year 1494. It was the time of the Tainos, a time when life seemed simpler, but Ana knew that all of that was about to change.

The Pull Of Freedom- Even in bondage the people, freshly arrived from Africa, considered themselves free. Led by Nanny and Cudjoe the slaves escaped the Simmonds' plantation and went in different directions to forge their destiny in the new country called Jamaica.

Jamaican Comedy (Material contains Jamaican dialect)

***Di Taxi Ride And Other Stories*-** Di Taxi Ride and Other Stories is a collection of twelve witty and fast paced short stories. Each story tells of a unique slice of Jamaican life.